Illustrated by David Tazzyman
The
ORPHANS of
ST HALIBUT'S
Sophie Wills
MACMILLAN CHILDREN'S BOOKS

First published 2020 by Macmillan Children's Books
an imprint of Pan Macmillan
The Smithson, 6 Briset Street, London EC1M 5NR
Associated companies throughout the world
www.panmacmillan.com

ISBN 978-1-5290-1337-5

1 3 5 7 9 8 6 4 2

A CIP catalogue record for this book is available from the British Library.

Printed and bound by CPI Group (UK) Ltd, Croydon CR0 4YY

For Fraser and Cameron

And in memory of Ken and Jenny Wills

To Little Buttcreak
To Lardidar Valley
Knott Wood
Ma Yeast's Bakery
St Cod's Home for Ingrates and Wastrels
The Mending House
Powders 'n' Potions Pharmacy

St Halibut's Home
for Waifs
and Strays
Pamela's
shed
Welcome to
Sad Sack

Prologue

When Herc woke up in the middle of the night, his first thought was of the cake, which had already been stolen twice. His second thought – that he had most definitely heard a noise downstairs – should probably have come first, but his brain had firm ideas about what sorts of things were important and there was no point in fighting it.

Something had smashed, and for once it *definitely* wasn't his fault.

Herc sat up and looked across the empty rows to the only other occupied bed in the dormitory, where Stef lay snoring, his finger rammed up one nostril as though plugging a leak in his head. Stef had asked Herc several times not to keep waking him in the night unless there was a real emergency. Apparently that didn't include wondering what the time was, needing a wee, having an itch, not even a nightmare. Herc always felt uneasy in the

darkness, seeing those other beds, because they had once contained his friends. It was like sleeping in a room full of ghosts.

He thought about getting Tig, who at twelve was a whole four years older and who would tell him not to be daft in the reassuringly cross way that only a big sister could. But she was all the way down the landing in the other dormitory – the only girl left in a room of what had once been twenty – and the floorboards between them squeaked, so he was afraid to tread on them. He was pretty sure the squeaks had been put there for exactly this reason.

The only other person left in the mansion that he might wake was the matron, Miss Happyday herself, and he didn't fancy being dangled out of the window by his hair again. Besides, it was she who had stolen the cake for the second time. Although she called it 'confiscating' and told him it was going in the bin. What was the point of stealing something if you were just going to throw it away?

The huge cake had been given to him by Ma Yeasty in the bakery, a free treat for her favourite orphans, but he had been robbed as he cradled it carefully home. The thief had been aiming for the whole cake and it was only due to Herc's whip-like reaction that her grasping hand had plunged through the middle of it instead. The girl had run off with her half-prize while Herc shouted after her, using words that weren't in any of Miss Happyday's dictionaries. He didn't need to follow the trail of crumbs to know where the crook in the yellow uniform lived: St Cod's. He hoped they'd all choke.

Herc hadn't even got past the front door of St Halibut's with the remaining half of the cake. Miss Happyday had spotted it behind his back the moment he'd returned home.

If anyone was going to steal it for a third time it was jolly well going to be him.

His bare feet made no sound on the stairs, and he could very clearly hear more noises below – heavy thuds, as though someone was throwing things around. A burglary? There was a lot of it about down in the town, that was for sure.

Off the back corridor downstairs, the kitchen door stood wide open. The sight that greeted him was devastating. He took in the plate, the two tiny crumbs, the shape of a finger having been swirled in the smear of chocolate icing and, no doubt, licked.

The empty plate confirmed it: now he was even more certain that there must be an intruder. Miss Happyday might have taken the half-cake from him, but she herself would never have eaten it. She was always telling them how unhealthy such things were. Whenever she found the children's hidden sweets, her eyes would widen in horror. The offending items would disappear into her pockets; he supposed she was too busy to throw them away immediately.

Another noise, a sort of scrabbling; it was coming from the library.

Now that the cake was gone, there was no real reason to hang about downstairs. But Herc had little use for reasons. If it turned out you needed any, you could always make them up afterwards.

He padded past the sour gazes of the wigged portraits in the hallway, and hesitated outside the library door. There was definitely a person in there. Someone was cackling and hiccupping at the same time. The oddest thing was, he recognized the voice, though he'd never heard her laugh before. It couldn't be . . .

'Miss Happyday?'

There was no answer. Only more thuds, another hideous cackle, and . . .

'Oooh ooh ah AHH!'

He frowned. Either the library had a monkey in it, or the matron doing an impression of one.

It struck him that Miss Happyday might not be quite well.

He turned the handle as gently as he could, opened

the door a tiny crack, and put his eye to it.

The rows of shelves stretching all the way to the ceiling stood in front of him like giant dominoes. Herc realized he had been quite wrong about Miss Happyday – she was plainly in excellent health. So excellent, in fact, that she was giggling, clinging to an upper shelf a dizzying distance from the ground, her stockinged legs bicycling in mid-air for something to rest on. He could see the path she had used to clamber to her current position, by the empty places where her sensible black boots had kicked books down to the floor.

Drawing in a sharp breath, Herc snapped the door closed again.

If Miss Happyday had taken up gymnastics, anything could happen.

He was just considering what to do about this when a shushing began from beyond the door, very much like the shushing the matron did when the children were breathing too loudly, but the sound grew in volume, as though the tide was coming in. The thuds became more frequent, a hailstorm drumming louder and louder, gathering strength.

Instinctively, Herc took a step back, as the floor under his feet began to shake and windows rattled in their frames. The crystal drops of the chandelier high above him tinkled, and then jangled and clashed. Several paintings fell to the ground behind him. The noise from inside the library was deafening, a thunder roll that echoed through his head and made Herc clap his hands to his ears. An earthquake? Was the whole house about to collapse? Just as suddenly as it had started, the noise began to die down, and then finally all was quiet.

Whatever had happened, it was over.

When he gathered the courage to open the door, it took him a moment to understand what he was seeing. Books. Which was not unusual in itself – this was the library, after all. But they were no longer on their shelves. They filled the room nearly to the top, a few slithering over his feet as the door swung open. Not a single one of the enormous shelves remained standing.

'Miss Happyday?' he called. 'Someone ate the cake you constipated. And, er, some books fell on the floor.' Silence. 'It wasn't me,' he added automatically.

He peered down at the textbooks covering his feet. There were several volumes of *Very Important Words to Learn*, a large hardback copy of *The Deadly Consequences of Poor Spelling* – the matron's favourite subject – and peeking out from underneath that was *The Joy of Fronted Adverbials*, its spine crushed and half hanging off, a muddy heel mark on the cover.

Tentatively he reached out and plucked one from the pile. It was another of Miss Happyday's favourites: *Fifty Thousand Little-Known Rules of Grammar* (subtitle: *You're Getting It All Wrong*). When Herc saw a familiar tightly laced boot revealed underneath it, he felt sure Stef and Tig wouldn't mind being woken up.

This was no nightmare.

Far from it.

Chapter One

Two months later

Tig stood on the driveway of St Halibut's Home for Waifs and Strays, watching the dot that was Maisie the postmistress increase in size as it lumbered towards her up the steep, winding path with their mail. As ever, she marvelled at the dedication of the woman who risked a heart attack by climbing all the way up here every time the orphanage had a single item of post, even if it was just a flyer for one of Ma Yeasty's regular bakery sales (ten per cent off any muffins more than six months old). If it were Tig's job, she'd let the letters build up for a couple of weeks and then send one of the town kids to deliver them for her, with the promise of a shiny halfpenny. She allowed herself a small smile. It wasn't as if she was short of halfpennies anymore. And Maisie could keep her job – she, Herc and Stef weren't ever going to need one. Just as long as they kept their mouths shut.

A chilly breath of wind lifted her hair and cut a shiver down her back. She wrapped her arms closer about her and eyed the fog that had gathered over the woods below. It crouched over the uppermost branches of the trees, its misty fingers stretching out greedily, now stroking the very edge of Sad Sack. Soon the town would be almost invisible in its grip, which would improve the view from St Halibut's no end.

The town of Sad Sack resembled nothing so much as a splodge of something unpleasant that should have been mopped up but, left to moulder, had eventually evolved its own life forms. The other local orphanage, St Cod's Home for Ingrates and Wastrels, festered near its centre, its residents feeding off the unguarded pockets of townsfolk like leeches. The bakery, the library, the butcher's, the pharmacy that sold incense and strange herbal medicines and smelt so thickly perfumed that the air inside the shop was almost solid in your throat – all were crammed into the winding cobbled streets in haphazard rows that looked like they might fall down if you laid a finger on one of them. But it was the huge Mending House next to St Cod's that dominated everything. Its stone walls formed a square with one missing side; tall iron railings and gates joined the open section, making a courtyard at the front. It squatted fat and menacing, its bleak chimneys casting murky shadows over all who lived there, the darkness seeming to spread from within its very walls. Tig did not like to look at it.

From the town, the grey stone mansion of St Halibut's looked the same as it always had – she'd made sure of that. It was beautiful in an unwelcoming sort of way. The same theme continued inside – high ceilings and great big sash windows and old paintings of gammon-faced jowly geezers, all designed to suggest that you weren't really posh enough to gaze upon it, let alone live there. Miss Happyday had floated about inside, the lady of the manor, as though she and the house were both in denial about the fact that it was also home to scruffy orphans. No one ever ascended the rickety stone steps that led up the steep hillside, apart from Maisie, and occasionally Arfur, who described himself as a travelling curiosity salesman, though he neither travelled much, nor sold anything worth being curious about. Tig knew what he really was, of course: a total slimeball.

Both visitors always came on foot, since the route up had not been fit for horse nor carriage for hundreds of years. It took a good twenty minutes to make the climb, even if you were fit and didn't stop to catch your breath, and the entire path was in full view of the sweeping drive, so the children were always forewarned of any approach. It was much faster on the way down, as Arfur had once demonstrated when he was drop-kicked off the driveway by Miss Happyday.

Today, Maisie's good-natured face was as rosy as ever from her exertions. She frequently insisted that each delivery might be her last – not, as Tig suspected, because the hill was going to kill her, but because she had big plans to set up her own knitting business. She'd been delivering the mail for more than twenty years, and had been threatening to stop for nineteen of them. She often brought up her spectacularly garish handmade scarves, socks and hats for the orphans, worrying that they were constantly in danger of hypothermia and needed to be wrapped in as many layers as possible.

'Love letter for your Miss Happyday, no doubt,' she told Tig with a wink as she handed over a buff envelope.

The ridiculousness of this idea always raised a smile, no matter that it was an old joke now. If ever the matron of St Halibut's had attracted feelings of love, they'd been vaporized on contact.

'Haven't seen her for an age, and it's just as well, far as I'm concerned, love. Hope she's not getting you and the other little ones down?'

'Not at all.'

'Ghastly, obnoxious woman. Don't give her my regards, will you?'

'I won't,' Tig promised as usual.

It was true that the matron was both ghastly and obnoxious, but she could be given no regards even if Maisie had wished it. The last thing she'd been given was two months ago, and that was a good, deep burial under the vegetable garden. The children had even chosen a suitable funeral hymn for the graveside, though it had probably never been intended to be sung quite so cheerfully as it was that day.

'You keep nice and warm now, in this weather. And make sure that little brother of yours wears his socks. That fog is bitter cold,' Maisie instructed.

Tig shrugged. 'It won't bother us up here.' Very little did, anymore.

The matron's death in the freak library collapse had been a shock at first, naturally. Herc claimed that the reason all the shelves had fallen on top of her was that she had been climbing them, but he'd clearly made that up. The only other theory was an earthquake, but that seemed just as unlikely. Why she'd even been there in the middle of the night was also a mystery. But before long the orphans had started calling it the Happy Accident, and after the unfortunate woman's secret funeral, a shadow lifted from St Halibut's. It was as though for the first time in the children's lives, the sun had come out, and they had not until that moment realized they had existed in darkness. A week later, they buried all the hated textbooks too, in a grave even deeper than that of Miss Happyday.

Though Tig wasn't quite the oldest – that was Stef – it was she who, in the first days of chaos after the death of the matron, had pointed out that their survival depended on bringing some tasks back into their lives, and suggested what might need doing. But it would never be like the matron's old Schedule; on that they were all agreed. No more spelling tests at 5 a.m., no more 'playtimes' spent ironing the matron's knickers and folding them with the help of a ruler and a ten-step diagram.

After some discussion they had decided it would be best not to rely entirely on trips down to Sad Sack for food, and so the vegetable garden was cared for as it had been before, but anything the children now found to be non-essential was ditched. As time went on, that included the reciting of times tables, the study of grammar, the washing of clothes, the using of cutlery, the making of beds, the brushing of hair and the tidying or cleaning of almost anything. Where once there had been a girls' dormitory and a boys' dormitory, they now fell asleep wherever took their fancy. After a wild few weeks of dragging their blankets on to window sills, into the porch and under the kitchen table, they had mostly decided beds were more comfortable, though they arranged them at awkward angles just because Miss Happyday would have been enraged to see them that way.

There was one exception to the general lack of rules, and that was that anyone going down to Sad Sack for supplies must look vaguely presentable to avoid arousing suspicion. On no account could any adult have the slightest inkling that all was not as it should be up on the hill. Even those few who seemed friendly, like Maisie, must be kept strictly in the dark. And so a bath would be filled, a comb found, and a grey St Halibut's uniform scrubbed and pressed for the occasion, holes darned. The school hat – there was only one tattered example remaining, the others having been used variously for catching cricket balls, nesting birds, and in one case, eaten – was donned before finally each mission to Sad Sack could be undertaken. Usually this job fell to Stef.

Stef, at twelve, was large for his age – thickset and taller than some adults – with hair that looked blue-black indoors but turned chestnut in sunlight. A vivid scar ran from just under his nose, across his mouth, down his chin and all the way to his neck. He had arrived as a two-year-old with this injury, after a tragic horse-and-carriage accident in which he was the only survivor. It had been Miss Happyday who had taken out a needle and thread and sewn Stef's face back together, resentment seeping from her every pore. 'Typical of them to give me the blemished ones,' she had said as she pressed her lips into a thin line, her needle going in and out in a fury, all her frustration sewed into his hot, red, bawling face. 'At least you'll never have cause to be vain.' Like the others, Stef knew nothing of his parents, although he had gathered that neither was from Sad Sack. Complete strangers seemed to have opinions on the matter – he was frequently asked where he was from and what sort of a name Stef was supposed to be, even once when he was standing in the bakery right next to Ma Yeasty, a woman named after a fungus.

Since Miss Happyday's untimely demise, Stef had been the only one to occasionally take a bath, filling the tub in the matron's en-suite bathroom with cold water and heating it with a stove of coals that she had fitted at vast expense for her own personal use. Therefore it was usually he who traipsed down to the town and bought meat from the butcher, tins of beans from the grocer, and more importantly the illegal – and expensive – sweets and biscuits that a few shopkeepers kept secretly under the counter, their sugar content being above the government-approved level.

There was plenty of money, since Miss Happyday turned out to have hoarded a great stash of banknotes under her bed, despite having always complained that she was poor. They'd always known this was nonsense – she clearly had enough to keep herself in comfort, and to keep the house in decent repair. But they were shocked to find that she had been sleeping on top of nearly ten thousand pounds, the sneaky old bat. It was enough to keep the three children in more sherbet lemons and pear drops than they could possibly eat for years to come.

And so, from the outside, St Halibut's was still your average sinister-looking mansion dedicated to the care and training of abandoned and orphaned children. But on the inside, and in the grounds behind, there was exuberant chaos. It would have given any visitor the kind of shock they could normally only expect if they stood on the roof in a thunderstorm waving an electric eel.

As Maisie was plodding back down the hill, Tig opened the letter and went very still.

What had come in the post was not just an envelope with a message in it. It was the most hideous possible combination of words ever set in ink. A ticking bomb wrapped in horse manure and chucked through the window would have been far more welcome.

Tig held it pinched between her thumb and forefinger, the stiff breeze snapping at the paper as though impatient to dispose of it. She imagined letting go, watching the wind snatch it high over the driveway and the expressionless dark windows of St Halibut's Home for Waifs and Strays.

She had been a fool to think their happiness would last for long. Three days: that was all that was left of their lives.

She barely heard Stef crunch up the gravel behind her. 'What's up?'

There were no words to express the horror.

'Tig?'

She turned and handed Stef the letter, her jaw clenched.

'DEATH is coming.'

Chapter Two

It was said that DEATH – the Department for Education, Assimilation, Training and Health – came to everybody in the end. It had been set up by the government with the noblest of aims: to ensure a peaceful population, and an end to all wars. Who could disagree?

Everybody knew that there were two basic causes to all arguments: 1) having opinions on things, and 2) having too much time on your hands. Therefore, it was much safer to rely only on Official Facts, and to occupy your mind with trivial things. That way, there would be no time to worry about the big awkward questions. Many of the sanctioned facts from DEATH were based on scientific evidence – such as the fact that it was healthier to eat vegetables and exercise than it was to guzzle butter straight out of the tub while remaining in bed.

Sometimes, however, science said things that were inconvenient, and when this happened, better facts were designed and paid for. For example, the prime minister's husband owned a company that sold radioactive health products – necklaces to cure rheumatism, blankets for arthritis, drinks for energy. Unfortunately, top doctors discovered that these were extremely bad for you, so those doctors were sacked, and different ones hired. The new doctors said, actually the facts *proved* that drinking radioactive water not only made you feel younger and put a spring in your step, but also that the strange buzzing light you started to emit was, in fact, a healthy glow.

Children were taught at home by their parents from a series of DEATH-issued textbooks, since it was unwise to encourage large gatherings of such dangerous and unpredictable creatures as under-thirteens. The exceptions to this were orphans, where it couldn't be helped. The government regularly sent agents of DEATH to inspect every orphanage in the country, to ensure that the children's brains were being filled with harmless things like the twenty-three times table, and made-up rules about the order of words in a sentence. Any child whose behaviour proved troublesome – whether reported by an orphanage matron, or even just a member of the public – would spend a short period in a local Mending House. Here they would alternate between hard physical work and advanced training in Pedantics, until they were exhausted but could punctuate any sentence in their sleep. Then they would be spewed out again, dazed, head full of facts that were useful for nothing except boring other people with.

It was all for their own good. DEATH had created this genius system to guarantee the general happiness of an entire population; it was just unfortunate that, on the whole, it made specific individuals very, very miserable.

And of course, although they tried, they didn't *always* know exactly what everyone was up to.

The Mending House of Sad Sack did not attract much attention, and that was how its governor, Ainderby Myers, liked it. Before he had taken over, ten years ago, it had functioned much the same as any other Mending House: child in, child Mended, child out again. But under his ownership, things had taken a far darker turn.

Visitors were forbidden now, the stone walls impenetrable and cold as the grave. Nothing was known of Ainderby Myers himself, except that he was very rich and that it was bad news if he noticed you. He never left the Mending House, though he could very occasionally be spotted stalking across the courtyard, or at the gate signing for parcels. And everyone knew he had loyal spies all over town.

While Ainderby Myers seemed to know about

everything that went on in Sad Sack, he did not welcome the same scrutiny for himself. Maisie, who – on account of her job – was one of the very few people to see him regularly, had once asked, 'And how are you, Mr Myers?' while handing over the post, and reckoned it no coincidence that the very same evening her house was raided by DEATH and her secret stash of cake and chocolate confiscated. Ever since, she had called down curses upon him – very quietly, in the privacy of her own home, when her cat was out, because you can't trust cats. But sadly, as her only weapon was delivering his mail, the most she could hope for was that he'd get a nasty paper cut from opening it.

Even in the bad old days of Miss Happyday, the orphans of St Halibut's consoled themselves that at least they weren't in the Mending House. In the orphanage they had enough to eat, and there was a fire in winter; Miss Happyday liked her home comforts, and to her annoyance it was impossible to stop them from accidentally benefitting the children. Her lessons were of the mind-numbing kind that involved repeating things over and over until you found your mouth could say them without any input from your brain, but nobody doubted that this was a thousand times better than whatever went on in the Mending House these days.

Officially, what went on in there was that cotton was spun and woven by children until their wayward souls were cured. Since Myers had taken over, it seemed the remedy was a long time coming: while cotton was released from the iron gates from time to time, no child ever was. All that ever escaped were faint despairing cries, and the kind of rumours that made you wish you'd never asked.

It was the Mending House that had swallowed up so many of the orphans who had once slept in the dormitories of St Halibut's. Once, the orphanage halls had echoed with the feet of more than forty children, hurrying to keep to Miss Happyday's strict Schedule (lessons of an hour each, two minutes for a wee at specific times of the day, two and a half minutes three times a week for anything more time-consuming). Then slowly, one by one, they each found themselves sentenced to Mending. The Guvnor's easily recognizable looped handwriting would appear on a white envelope on the doormat, a summons. Every time she saw one, the matron was consumed by outrage. Myers already had plenty of children, she thundered, without stealing hers on some made-up pretext, such as that they'd been throwing stones at the Mending House windows. Even St Cod's had more children than she did now, and the matron there – Miss Lackspittle – appeared to be teaching a lot more pickpocketing than grammar.

Miss Happyday had known better than to complain to DEATH, however. Praised and respected as a matron she might be, and a terrifying force in her own right, but she still knew her limits. Ainderby Myers was very popular with DEATH, because his paperwork was immaculate: his accounts always added up, and his records – of meals taken, height and weight of each Mended child, dates of entry – were compiled into beautifully symmetrical colour-coded charts which made his bosses sigh with pleasure. Anyone who produced such things clearly needed no one looking over his shoulder. A click of his fingers and Miss Happyday would be given the sack. Not just given it, either, but weighed down and sent to the bottom of the river in it by one of the Guvnor's hired thugs. And so, white-lipped with fury, she would shove each condemned child out of the door into the waiting arms of Myers' guards, and only spit and swear once they were well out of earshot. In the past two years alone, Mary, Seema, Clarry and Eric had all passed through the door, never to return again.

Always, she took out her rage on the remaining children. Just because she wanted more, it didn't mean she liked having them; she liked the *payment* she got from

DEATH for having them. And fewer orphans meant less cash. She wanted her private wing of the house to look elegant, and all those antique ornaments and plush rugs didn't come cheap.

But then, shortly before her death, when Miss Happyday was down to only three remaining orphans to watch over – Tig, Herc and Stef – the matron began to swagger around the mansion with an ugly expression that could only be described as smug. The children had no idea what to make of it.

'There'll be no more envelopes from that swindling Guvnor,' she said to her remaining charges. 'Ever again. And I'm applying for some new orphans.'

Shortly afterwards, the Happy Accident meant that the appropriate form was only half filled, never sent and there would be no new orphans at St Halibut's.

But now DEATH was coming to inspect them, which meant that, barring a miracle, there would very soon be no orphans there of any kind.

Chapter Three

Stef, opposite Tig at the kitchen table, looked as though he might faint when Tig went through the full details of the inspection. His chest was rising and falling as though his heart and lungs were fighting to get out of his ribcage. He was probably going to be sick, which was his usual reaction to anything scary. Tig smothered a flash of irritation. Why was it always *her* keeping things together? She jerked her eyes meaningfully to indicate that Stef should put on a calm front for her younger brother.

She needn't have worried.

'YES! A visitor! Finally!' yelled Herc, pumping his fist.

'Uh, yeah.' She glanced back at Stef, hunched over as though a DEATH inspector might swoop in over his head at any moment. 'Mm, that's nice, isn't it? So we just have to convince the inspector that everything's completely normal. Give him a good time. Make him feel like we're on top of things here. Then he'll go away again.'

Stef's mouth dropped open. 'Give him a good time? You're not serious. We have to *leave.* Right now.'

Tig leaned across the table and hissed quietly in his face, resisting the urge to shake him. 'I'm not saying it'll be easy. But we have nowhere to go, except some other Home. And that means a matron.'

He hesitated. 'I know, but—'

'We've been happy the last few weeks. Doing whatever we want, eating whatever we want. And Herc . . . he'd never have another birthday cake . . .'

They turned to Herc, who, momentarily distracted, was drawing a picture with his finger in a puddle of week-old soup on the table. He tended to live in the moment. He had probably already forgotten the matron's approach to their growing older, which was that since the orphans belonged to her, so did their birthdays. As a result, she had celebrated her own birthday once a week, while the children were forbidden from mentioning theirs. Tig had once observed to the matron that this would explain why she appeared to be ageing so quickly, and received a whipping for her trouble.

A couple of days after the matron's death, Tig and Stef had helped Herc to make his first-ever birthday cake, and his joy had been so huge, his happiness so warming to behold, that they had since given him a birthday celebration every time they felt like it. Watching him blow out the candles and wolf down his cake made everything seem better, somehow. In the last two months, Herc had had forty-six birthdays.

Tig pressed her point, moving round to sit on the table right by Stef, speaking low. 'Come on. You know we can't run away. The only reason we've been safe so far is that we're isolated up here. Anywhere else, we'd soon have people noticing that no one's looking after us.'

'Maybe you're right. But how can we pass an inspection? We haven't spelled so much as our own names for weeks.'

'We'll have to spell things?' Suddenly Herc sounded worried. Any visitor who made him spell was never going to be his friend. He considered himself a very talented speller, but the dictionary always disagreed with him, and everyone always took the dictionary's side.

'We can do it,' Tig reassured him. 'It'll all come back to us.'

Stef was rubbing at his forehead. 'Even if it does . . . look around you.' he gestured at the kitchen floor, covered in covered in the detritus from the previous months' dinners. When Tig moved, her boot clung briefly to a sticky patch that had been there for weeks. 'If he has eyes, this . . .' he checked the letter on the table – 'Inspector Kirkby Fleetham will know as soon as he comes through the front door that something's not right.'

Tig shrugged impatiently. 'So, we clean up. We have three days.'

'It's not just that. He'll want to talk to us. *All of us.*' Stef deliberately did not look at Herc.

'We'll practise what to say,' insisted Tig. 'None of us will give the game away. And we'll check what we're supposed to have been doing and cram it. I'm sure we'll race through it once we get back into the Schedule.'

A horrified squeak came from Herc. 'Not the Schedule! You promised we'd never do it again!'

'I know. I'm sorry. But we have to, otherwise we won't fool any inspector for a second.' They were more than rusty. 'It's Tuesday now. The inspection is on Friday morning. We can put up with it for that long.'

Stef shook his head. 'You're forgetting the most obvious thing. He'll expect to see Miss Happyday. What are you going to do, dig her up?'

They all shuddered.

'We'll say she had to pop out urgently, and won't be back till he's gone. The inspection'll only last a few hours. He won't be able to do anything about it.'

Herc giggled excitedly. 'Yeah! He'll think it's the best orphanage he's ever seen, the sucker!'

Tig thumped him gently on the head. 'That's exactly the kind of thing you won't be able to say.'

Stef sniffed lightly. 'Herc . . . can you go and grab me a hanky from my drawer? I think I'm getting a nosebleed.'

'Have you been picking your nose again?' Herc admonished him. Stef's nosebleeds were legendary – years of picking his nose meant that the blood vessels inside were delicate, and at times of stress sent forth an unstoppable flow. 'Tig said if you poke too far, your brains can come out of your ears.' He leaned up close to Stef's nose as if considering crawling up it to see. 'If it does, will you show me? I don't want to miss it.'

They listened to the sound of Herc scampering up the stairs like a herd of elephants. Stef's voice was strained. 'Tig . . . if we fail . . . *when* we fail . . . you know what they'll do to us. Where we'll go.'

She knew. They both knew. The fear in Stef's voice seemed to take solid form and come alive; they could feel its breath on their necks.

Tig turned up the collar of her cardigan. 'We won't fail. We can't.'

Chapter Four

That evening, snow began to fall over Sad Sack. It fell in thick flakes that clung to roof tiles and doorsteps and soon covered the cobbled streets. On any other town it might have been picturesque, but here its sparkle was frozen and cruel. It hid none of the ugliness of the huddled-together houses with their missing roof tiles and cracked windows. The Mending House was the only building largely free of snow – the broad middle section was the factory itself, where the air had to be kept warm and moist at all times, to keep the fragile cotton yarn from breaking as it was spun.

There was one end of the roof where the snowflakes had not melted. This end had the thickest blanket of snow in Sad Sack and under it lay the dormitory of the Mended. Ainderby Myers liked to say that because they had been in the heat of the factory all day, they had no need of warmth at night. If you passed down the side alley between St Cod's and the Mending House late at night, you could hear endless hacking coughs echoing off the stone walls like pistol shots.

The Guvnor's quarters were at the opposite end of the building, and here a pleasant fire was burning. Then it flickered and a draught of freezing air across the back of his neck told Ainderby Myers that someone was behind him in his study. For the tiniest of moments he felt fear, but he immediately snuffed it out, like crushing the delicate flicker of a candle between finger and thumb. You had to do it fast, or the flames would take hold. Besides, he knew who it was. He'd been expecting him.

He gripped the silver letter opener in his fist, having just opened yet another infernal envelope from Lady Crock, his boss at DEATH, who was a world-class numpty. This latest message was a thick wad of paper wanting to know whether his punctuation targets had been met in the classes he was supposed to hold for the Mended, but obviously never did. She wanted him to answer row upon row of tedious questions, such as whether apostrophes had been used correctly 'all of the time', 'most of the time', some of the time', 'rarely' or 'never'. It would take all of his self-control not to add another line at the bottom saying 'Does Lady Crock deserve to be tortured with red-hot pokers under her fingernails while lying in a bath full of leeches?' and tick 'all of the time'. He suspected before long she'd want him to fill in a form justifying what style of underpants he planned to wear each morning and detailing the exact shade on a colour chart. He had never met her, but was subjected to a constant stream of pointless demands from her office, the replies to which probably went straight into her bin unread. He was meticulous with it, despite this, because it meant she would keep her beak out of his business.

'Can't you knock?' he snapped, not giving his visitor the courtesy of turning around.

There was a short silence, and then two slow, sarcastic raps on the wood of the open door. Not like the knocks of the Mended – theirs were faint, as though made by the beak of a tiny, frail bird. This had some swagger to it; someone was getting above themselves.

Myers knew that Snepp didn't appreciate being summoned like some kind of servant, that the guards had been teasing him about it. Well, boohoo. If Snepp thought he could get cheeky and sneak up on him to make a point, it was about time he learned a lesson.

The letter opener left his hand and, *thunk*, had buried its blade in the door even before the knock had died away. There was a sharp intake of breath and only now did Myers turn in his chair to check out the result.

Snepp, shifted his gaze very slowly away from the quivering knife handle a splinter's width from his cheek. His throat bobbed as it struggled to swallow. Myers approached him and stood very close, as Snepp tried not to meet his stare; up close the Guvnor's face was always a shock. Myers was far younger than most people expected – perhaps thirty, if that – but in his eyes were several lifetimes, and not pleasant ones, either.

Myers enjoyed a smidgeon of satisfaction – he liked to give nightmares to people who normally gave nightmares to other people – but almost immediately felt it drain away. It wasn't enough anymore.

And neither was the money.

It was DEATH's own fault that he had been forced to find other ways to get the kind of wealth he wanted. It wasn't as if they paid him much, and the cotton mill was not profitable. At least, not enough for him.

His burglary team was hand-picked from among the Mended: hard-working, relatively healthy and disposable. They never stayed healthy for long – a result of the dust they worked in all day, which clogged up their lungs, and the regular accidents in the factory – so he was constantly having to replace them. None of this was evident from the paperwork, of course. And he always had Snepp get rid of them before it was too late, so as to avoid the cost of coffins. If anyone was nearby when they were carried out the side door, he'd tell Snepp loudly to take them to hospital, but they both knew he meant 'I don't care if you throw them off a cliff'.

Instead of sleeping at night, selected Mended would be shinning up drainpipes, slipping through windows and picking locks, returning with treasures for his vault. Since the 'hospitalization' of yet another burglar, he currently had only one left – Ashna; but she was brilliant. He never usually bothered to learn the names of the Mended, but she was special. Unfortunately she'd already lost a fingers from her right hand in the spinning mule by the time he identified where her real talents lay, but it didn't seem to have hindered her. His vault was stuffed with the treasures she had pilfered. He could sense the reassuring weight of them in the room above him. Normally the thought of it comforted him. Today he was only aware of what was missing.

'I have a special job for you,' he told his visitor. 'It has been set up with a great deal of care and precision, and now it's ready.'

Snepp said nothing. He had been given 'special jobs' by Myers many times before, and they usually involved violence. He was OK with that.

'I need you to retrieve something that belongs to me. Something that was . . . lost.'

Snepp's mouth pursed in disappointment – what, he was a lost-property clerk now? – but he remained silent. He, of all people, knew not to offer unwelcome opinions to his master. It had been his job to tie a knot in the tongue of the last person who had done that.

'And when you've got it, I want you to bring me the people responsible.'

All right. That was more like it.

Chapter Five

Under Miss Happyday, every minute of every day had dragged.

Now, of all weeks, Time had chosen this one to start sprinting so fast that Tig felt breathless trying to keep up.

It was already Wednesday, and she wasn't sure St Halibut's looked any different from how it had looked the day before. They were all mucking in. Even Herc had been flapping damp cloths around the furniture in an effort to remove the thick coatings of dust. It wasn't happening fast enough, though. They had once been so good at cleaning – now it seemed they had forgotten how to use a broom or a cloth without either poking someone else in the eyeball or flooding the floor. The mess was just moving around rather than reducing.

The Schedule was back in place, sort of. They'd made a decent bash at two-minute teeth-brushing, though afterwards there was more toothpaste on the floor than could possibly have ended up in anyone's mouth, and only Tig remembered to tick the box on the wall chart afterwards.

Tig and Herc sat wrapped in their knitted layers on a rug on the snow-covered grass, cramming as much textbook information into their memories as possible, so that it could be retrieved from their brains and offered up to the inspector like a sacrifice, as their matron would have expected.

Stef had a theory that Miss Happyday had been Mended long ago, which would explain her unthinking loyalty to DEATH and the Schedule. But Tig didn't buy it. Not only did she have trouble imagining Miss Happyday ever having been a wayward child in need of Mending, but the matron did not have the blank stare and empty eyes of the Mended. She enjoyed her power over the children, and punished them with a passion and intensity that fed her soul. The Mended of Sad Sack were said to know no enjoyment, or desire. Those feelings were taken from them when they entered the gate of the Mending House, along with their worldly possessions. They just did as they were told. Tig and Stef tried not to talk about their old friends who had suffered this fate, not just because it was too painful, but in case it upset Herc.

He had stopped asking questions about them some time ago, since nobody had any answers, but Tig knew that didn't mean he wasn't thinking about them.

Tig was poring over *Who Needs Friends When You Have Semi-Colons?* its pages stained and filthy from its recent burial, while Herc had dug through the snow and was absent-mindedly ripping fistfuls of grass from the lawn with one hand, a vocabulary list in the other, in an effort to learn something, anything.

Tig had some sympathy with him. He was not a natural academic. He now spent his days running around the house and gardens making secret dens, performing alarming scientific experiments and shouting to imaginary friends until he was hoarse, while she unsuccessfully tried to keep an eye on him. Although it had been years since there had been anyone here near his own age, he had blossomed, despite Miss Happyday's best efforts. He was ingenious in creating his own games, inquisitive and enthusiastic about everything.

She couldn't help worrying about how Herc would fare during the inspection. He was a terrible speller, for a start, despite his unshakeable confidence in his own ability. Even through years of Miss Happyday's constant criticisms, Herc's self-belief was unquenchable. It was a running joke between Tig and Stef that there was nothing

Herc couldn't do, from pole-vaulting to brain surgery.

'Listen,' she told him now. 'This is really important. Don't give away any secrets to the inspector, and don't let on that there's anything in Miss Happyday's room – that's where we're going to hide stuff we don't want him to see, right? He mustn't know there's anything in there. Oh, and the library – it's locked because it's being redecorated. Got it?' They had not even attempted to fix the huge shelves. But perhaps she should keep it simple for him: 'Just don't tell him anything or show him anything.'

'OK, OK. Can I stop?' Herc asked Tig. 'My brain is itchy. And I'm already brilliant at it.'

'Let's just test you on a few words. How about . . .' She scanned her memory for vocabulary at his level. He ought to be on level 2.6 of *Very Important Words to Learn*, she thought. 'Tell me what these words mean, OK? We'll start with something easy . . . "artery".'

Herc grinned at her. 'Oh that *is* easy. That's like, a place where there are lots of paintings. Art-ery.'

'Uh, well . . . OK, let's try a really short one. What does "bide" mean? As in, "to bide your time".'

Herc didn't hesitate. 'It's when you get something with money, but you did it earlier. Like, "He bide sweets yesterday." Or, "He couldn't think of an example, so he bide time."'

Tig took a breath to correct him, looked into his eager face, and let the breath out again. What was the point? 'Good work, Herc. Carry on.'

She left him and headed back into the house, ducking under the sagging wooden lintel over the door. That was another thing that needed fixing, but she'd have to ask Stef to do it; he was the only one strong enough. And there were too many other things for her to do, like lugging all their stuff up the stairs into Miss Happyday's room – she'd never realized quite how many comics Herc had acquired in such a short time.

They still had a day and a half. It was enough time. It would have to be.

One thing was for sure, though. Whatever happened, they would have to keep Herc well away from the inspector.

Chapter Six

'Wass all this, then?'

Tig's head thwacked the underside of one of the tables in the hallway as she jumped in shock at Arfur's voice just behind her. She'd been trying to scrub away some unidentifiable stain that refused to budge.

'What are you doing in here?' She could have kicked herself. Stef was in town buying supplies, and she'd been so busy she hadn't thought to keep a check on the path up the hill. If Arfur sussed that something was going on, they'd be done for. He'd sell his granny if he could get the right price – sell her, steal her back, and sell her again to the same poor sap who'd bought her in the first place, claiming she was new and improved.

'Left the door open, didn't you? Oughta be careful, doing that. Never know who might turn up.'

'So I see. You can't just walk in here, you know.'

Arfur blinked innocently. 'It's only little old me. Spotted your mate in town just now, the big fella. Looked all stressed out, like he had something on his mind, you know?' His gaze slid around the still-messy entrance hall, taking in the scattered papers on the floor where Herc had been drawing cartoons instead of tidying.

Herc had been obsessed with comics ever since Arfur had secretly brought him a tattered, ancient one called *Max und Moritz* in return for a penny – the words were in a language none of them understood, but the pictures were clear enough: two boys playing ghastly tricks on people. Herc found it hilarious, but Tig had been cross with Arfur – Herc hardly needed any more encouragement to get up to mischief, and if the matron had found it she'd have blown her top. Fiction had been allowed under Miss Happyday, but it hadn't been read; rather it was mined for verbs, or subordinate clauses, or whatever the subject of the day was, these nuggets dutifully piled and counted. It had come as a delightful surprise to Herc that novels actually had stories in them, though he preferred his penny comics, stashed under a floorboard beneath his bed.

'This place isn't at all how I thought it would be inside,' Arfur was saying airily as Tig attempted to push him back out of the door, without success.

A small, wiry, rat-like man, Sad Sack's resident swindler had staying power. His wary eyes shifted constantly in search of opportunities to make a quick profit.

Once, astonishingly, he had been married to Maisie the postmistress, but they no longer spoke, and she reacted to any mention of his name as though it were something she'd stepped in. He sold brand-new watches that only worked for about five minutes after purchase, compasses that stubbornly insisted north was south, and other useless knick-knacks that had probably very recently belonged to someone who didn't yet know they'd disappeared.

Considering the poor quality of most of his merchandise, he was remarkably successful in persuading people to part with their money. He and Miss Happyday, however, had not got along, although for his part he always treated her with a fawning politeness, dropping flattery and compliments from his lips like coins into a music box. But the matron was not to be played. Perhaps it took a crook to know a crook, but she was not for an instant taken in by his sales patter. Nevertheless, he was back week after week, stubborn as a ketchup stain on her best tablecloth, almost as though he enjoyed annoying her. Or was snooping.

After that time she had sent him tumbling down the

hill from a well-placed boot to his backside, no one had expected to see Arfur again, since his body must surely have been dashed on the stones below. But the following week he had returned, with merely a limp and a better knowledge of the times that Miss Happyday would be out. No limbs were broken, not even a sprained wrist.

Right now, Tig was tempted to give it another try with her own boot.

'Get out, Arfur.'

'That's not very nice, Tig. You sound just like the matron.' His sharp eyes focused on her. 'Haven't seen *her* around for a very long time, now I come to think of it.'

'Lucky you. Now go, will you? We're not buying anything today. We're busy.'

She gave him another shove, but it was like nudging a wall.

'So I gather.' His lips formed a chummy smile. 'Funny thing is, I haven't seen hide nor hair of her for . . . ooh, weeks. Months, in fact.'

'Well, she's—'

'I keep an eye out, see? So as not to bump into her when it's inconvenient. I watch the comings and goings.' He walked his fingers up and down an imaginary hill.

The hairs on the back of Tig's neck began to prickle. 'You've just missed her.'

His smile grew, and he began to nod, as though at some private joke.

'But I don't think *you* have, have you? Missed her, I mean. You haven't missed Miss Happyday at all, far as I can tell. Don't blame you in the slightest.'

Tig's face was like stone. 'I don't know what you're talking about.'

'I reckon you do.'

There was a stand-off, which felt like it lasted for hours but must only have been seconds, in which the two of them faced each other, inches apart, Arfur's nose barely higher than Tig's. Finally she gave in.

'All right. Tell me what you think, you hideous weasel.'

The insult slid straight over his greasy hair. 'I think she's done a runner. Or dead. One of those. And –' He leaned in so close she could see the tiny red veins in the whites of his eyes – 'judging by the look on your face I'd say it's the latter. Was it . . . *murder?*'

There was an outraged gasp behind Tig as Herc appeared, picking up his drawings like a good boy. 'We wouldn't do that! It was an accident!'

Tig's eyes closed. It was a moment before she opened them again, because she couldn't bear to see the triumph on Arfur's loathsome mug.

He knew, and she knew, that he now had something worth paying for.

Chapter Seven

Stef had been glad of the excuse to get out of the house to go and buy bread earlier that morning. The atmosphere at St Halibut's was oppressive, stretched taut like the skin of a drum.

Their lives were pretty good right now. He liked tending to the vegetable garden, choosing what to grow and being responsible for doing the shopping. They had everything they needed. They even had their own milk now, since Stef had bought Pamela. The children had decided a cow would be a good idea, and Stef had been pleased – and a little nervous – that Tig tasked him with buying one, pretending to do so on behalf of the matron.

Unfortunately, before Stef had got halfway down the hill, let alone anywhere near a farm, Arfur had waylaid him and persuaded him that *he* could find the best cow, at the best price. To be fair, he was indeed offering one at a suspiciously low cost. But that wasn't the only thing that troubled Stef when Arfur turned up at the door with her the following day.

'Why's she wearing a muzzle?' Stef had asked.

'Dry lips,' explained Arfur without hesitation. 'Bit of moisturizer will sort that out. Her name's Pamela. A beauty, ain't she?'

Stef was frowning. 'She doesn't look right. She's a bit small.'

'Hush now,' Arfur had said, covering Pamela's ears. 'They do have *feelings*, you know.' A strange, muffled noise came from the muzzle.

'What was that?' said Stef, alarmed.

'Good grief, mate, don't you know nothing? That's a ruddy moo, innit. You want her or not?'

Stef had hesitated. Tig would kill him if he got this wrong, but he didn't want to check every tiny thing with her – it would make him look like he couldn't even handle a simple task. She was constantly telling him he was far too trusting of people, gullible even, but in his opinion the problem was that she suspected everyone.

'You're sure she's a good milker?'

Arfur gestured underneath Pamela. 'Got all the equipment, ain't she? Try it out. Yank on them dangly things.'

She did indeed have a set of udders in what was

probably the right place, but Stef had no idea how to get anything out of them. He thrust his hands in his pockets so hard he felt a seam rip.

Arfur sighed impatiently. 'Listen, take her or leave her but I'm only giving you this one chance, and at a knock-down price too. I'm practically robbing myself here, soft-hearted sap that I am. I'd take advantage if I were you. She's a rare breed, see? A White-Bearded Leghorn. One of a kind.'

Stef licked his lips. Maybe he should shop around a bit.

'Right you are. You tell your matron I got a long list of folks who'd bite me arm off for her.' Arfur turned to head away.

Stef made a decision. 'All right, all right. We'll take her.'

As Arfur set off down the hill with his payment, whistling, Stef tugged on Pamela's lead to take her round the back and show her where they'd prepared her nice cosy shed. Her body went rigid and her hooves dug into the grass.

While he was considering what to do about this, Tig's incredulous voice came from behind him. 'What on earth have you got there?' She stood at the door regarding Pamela, open-mouthed.

'Our cow. I know she's small, but she's a White-Bearded Leghorn,' he said knowledgeably.

Tig shook her head as she stared at him. 'Amazing. Stef, I underestimated you.'

Stef ducked his chin shyly. He had actually impressed her. 'Oh? Well, thanks. I told Arfur there must be no messing about, and for once I think he's taken me seriously.'

'He's certainly taken you for something. That's a goat.'

In the end, they kept Pamela. Arfur refused to give them a refund, adamant that goats and cows were practically the same species, and they were just splitting hairs.

She did at least produce milk. Stef wasn't sure how long it was going to keep coming out – he thought there must be some kind of important process behind it involving goat babies, but she didn't seem to be having any of those.

Arfur hadn't been lying about the fact that Pamela was unique: no one hated human beings more than she did. The muzzle had stopped her biting, as Stef had discovered to his cost when he took it off. Her horns were curved and sharp and, when she dipped her head, were at just the right angle to skewer you like a kebab. Maisie had taken to bringing a pair of binoculars with her up

the hill to check that the enclosure was securely fastened, before she would come anywhere near. When she heard they had bought Pamela from Arfur, she had shaken her head and said he always did keep bad company.

Their new goat did not merely dislike people. Pamela's hatred was a force greater than her body could contain. To look into her eyes was to experience depths of malevolence that must have been brewing since before the world began, a bitter hostility that would like to grind each tiny trace of humankind into dust. The fact that she needed humans to milk her, clear up her manure and feed her seemed only to fuel her anger.

Except for Herc. He was OK, apparently.

They couldn't figure out why Herc was the exception to Pamela's general rule. While the others would leave her shed with bite marks and bruises, Herc could change the hay, muck out and milk her while Pamela stood peacefully, submitting to his attentions and gently expelling gas so powerful that they considered bottling it and selling it as an offensive weapon.

They had fenced off a large area for Pamela to roam in, which she regularly broke out of in order to snaffle unharvested carrots from the vegetable garden. When she escaped, though, she showed no inclination to run off. Perhaps she realized what a good deal she had.

They all did.

Having reached Sad Sack, Stef now wondered if Pamela's constant filthy mood was because Arfur had taken her goat babies away before selling her, and was immediately overwhelmed by a soul-churning guilt so disturbing that he failed to pay attention to where he was going. He tripped over a sullen girl in the vomit-yellow uniform of St Cod's loitering just before the bakery, no doubt relieving passers-by of their wallets. The garish colour of the St Cod's uniform was useful, because it meant they could usually be spotted a mile off and avoided. Stef averted his eyes from her while trying to protect the four pockets of his trousers with only two hands. He could feel her contempt boring into the back of his head.

'Yeah, off you hop, snootypants,' she called after him. 'You've got nothing I want. Would've had it already if I did!'

Stef pursed his lips sourly, resisting the temptation to inform her that *actually* he had sixpence in his pocket, which just showed what *she* knew. It was shocking how Miss Lackspittle, the matron of St Cod's, let her charges get away with this kind of behaviour. She was so neglectful she made Miss Happyday look like a doting aunt. She was even rumoured to eat them, from time to time, when she noticed them. Unsurprisingly, Miss Lackspittle, like Miss Happyday, was required to give an orphan to the Mending House from time to time, but it did not seem to affect her laid-back attitude towards childcare. Myers could probably have taken them even if they were perfectly behaved.

Stef could smell Ma Yeasty's as he approached, and inhaled the heady scent of freshly baked loaves and warm dough rising under cloths. It was odd, he thought, that the aroma of her shop was so heavenly, because Ma Yeasty herself was as rank and foul-smelling a person as you could meet. Her personal habits were so disgusting and careless that it was not unusual to find hairs, toenails or a great matted wodge of belly-button fluff in the midst of your crusty wholemeal roll. A lot of people in Sad Sack chose to make their own bread. The orphans currently had other things on their minds, however; and they'd never been fussy.

Ma Yeasty would never be praised for her contribution to public health, unlike the unbearably smug greengrocer, Arty Chokes, who displayed his many awards for being a Provider of Very Healthy Food in his window. Her bakery operated just at the edge of what was considered to be nutritionally acceptable, and every day she ran the risk of being raided and shut down for supplying naughty treats to Sad Sackers. She claimed to use honey rather than sugar in her sweet products, since the mention of sugar made the inspectors come over all faint, and start fanning themselves. And while she did stock some suspiciously sweet scones, she made sure there were also plenty of broccoli muffins on display whenever DEATH came calling. Mostly she used them to hold open the door on hot days.

When Stef walked in, Ma Yeasty was shouting at someone, and waving her metal tongs around. The tongs were not in aid of hygiene, since she picked everything up with her grubby hands. The only thing he'd ever seen her use them for was a good old scratch under her sweaty armpit whenever she had fleas, which was constantly.

'Yes yer did, yer little beggar! I saw you! Put it back!'

The object of Ma Yeasty's rage was standing with his back to Stef: a thin boy dressed in the dreaded yellow shirt and ill-fitting trousers. His knees were knocking together either from cold or fear. The boy shook his head hard enough to make his brain rattle.

Ma Yeasty put her hands on her hips and belched powerfully over a tray of scones. A well-dressed lady, who had been reaching for one, abruptly changed her mind.

'I'm no mathematician but I can count. There was four cinnamon whirls right there on that tray and only two of them's left. That means you took . . .' Her lips moved silently while she did the calculations. 'Three and a half. Turn out yer pockets, yer rotter.'

The boy turned to flee but Ma Yeasty was quick as a flash with the tongs, and caught him by the collar of his shirt. While he wriggled and squirmed she fished about in his bulging pockets. A slightly squashed cinnamon whirl fell to the floor and she put her boot on it, as though it might run off.

'I knew it! Little weasel.'

With one mighty yank, the boy's shirt tore from his shoulders and he sprinted bare-chested to the door, barging roughly past Stef and out into the freezing air.

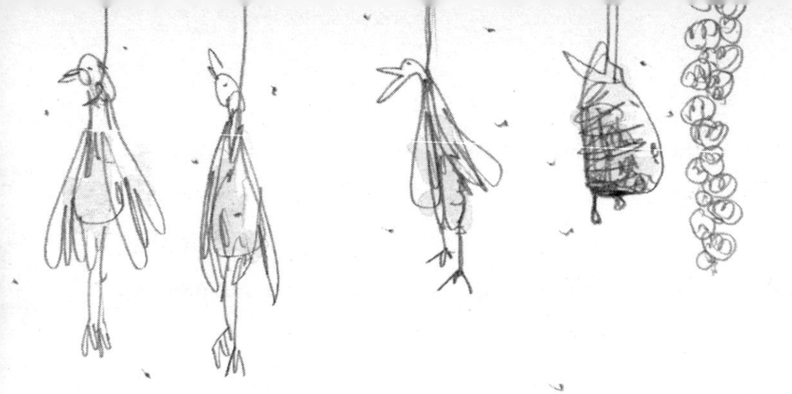

Ma Yeasty sniffed, then hawked and spat on the sawdust-covered floor, before bending to pick up the pastry from under her boot. 'Ooh, them St Cod's kids.' She caught sight of Stef and grinned. There was a crust of something stuck between her front teeth. 'Not like you nice St Halibut's young 'uns. What can I do you for?'

She'd always had a soft spot for Stef. Possibly because he was too polite to complain about the crusty toenails, unlike all her other customers.

'Oh!' Stef said suddenly, feeling in his pocket. 'My money's gone! He must have taken it when he ran out!'

She sniffed, unsurprised. 'Keep meaning to have a word with Miss Lackspittle about them, but she hasn't come in here ever since that misunderstanding with the dead mouse in her bap. Some people are right fusspots.' She sneezed forcefully, wiped her nose on a loaf and thumped it on the counter. 'Here, have this on the house and we'll say no more about it. Meant to ask, how did Herc like his cake?'

'Eh?' Stef was slightly distracted by an ooze of yellowy-green snot making its way down from her left nostril in a bid to join its companion on the loaf.

'That massive cake I gave him, ooh, couple months back. He's not been in since, so I wondered if maybe it was too rich for his little tummy. Only I put a lovely big lot of you-know-what in it. Special treat. I did tell him not to eat it all at once, course, or he'd be bouncing off the walls.'

'You-know-what' could mean many things in Sad Sack, including DEATH, Mending, spelling, sugar and money, which caused no end of confusion. The only possibilities here, Stef felt, were sugar or money, and even

Ma Yeasty surely wouldn't be so generous as to put cash in a cake.

'Er, probably.' It was hard to focus on what she was saying. The ooze had reached her top lip, and was hesitating. Possibly the smell of her breath was putting it off going any further. The meaning of Ma Yeasty's words was trundling slowly through Stef's brain like a badly chipped marble in a marble run, rolling and jerking inexorably downward. Herc had mentioned something about the matron stealing his cake before she died. Herc had not been bouncing off the walls, but Miss Happyday had. Or at least climbing them. Was it possible she had done so in a sugar-induced craze? It was well known that adults couldn't handle the stuff in large quantities.

Ma Yeasty was still rattling on. 'Thought I might try adding a few exotic herbs, from that Mr Brimstone in Powders 'n' Potions. Bit of an experiment, but I'm creative like that, me.'

'Hmm.' He watched as her tongue popped out from her lips and scooped up the trail of goo. He began to feel slightly sick. 'Ma Yeasty . . . Powders 'n' Potions doesn't sell herbs. Well, not ones for cooking with, anyway.'

She looked dumbfounded. 'It doesn't?'

'Um, no. Bickley Brimstone's a pharmacist. You know, he sells medicines.'

'Well, knock me down with a feather! All them years, I thought he was just a rubbish greengrocer. Can't bear that stuck-up Mr Choke so thought I'd try Mr Brimstone instead. What's all them dried-up old sticks, then?'

'That's incense, Ma Yeasty. You're meant to burn them, to make it smell nice.'

'Crikey. And here's me all that time, wondering if I should tell him his leeks is past their sell-by date.' She shook her head in disbelief at a world where people bought fancy knick-knacks and then set light to them. Stef tried not to think about what might happen if she started baking with Bickley Brimstone's products.

'Stick to sugar, I think.'

'SHHHHHHHHHHH!' Approximately half a pint of saliva sprayed across the room like rapid gunfire as she turned this way and that to check no one had heard him use the word. 'Here, want this? Another freebie.' She waved the crushed cinnamon pastry at him, now soggy with her spit, and indented neatly with the shape of her boot heel. But he was already out the door, looking slightly green, and retching.

'Wait! You forgot your loaf!' She sighed, and set it aside in case he remembered later. Always had half a mind elsewhere, that boy, and so often looked like he was about to puke – almost every time he was in her shop, it seemed.

The cinnamon pastry she pulled back into shape and set carefully back on the tray for the next customer. 'Waste not, want not.'

Stef hated going into Powders 'n' Potions – it was right opposite the Mending House, for a start – but there was a funny smell in the St Halibut's bathroom and he reckoned they could cover it up with one of Mr Brimstone's potent herb mixes if they burned it right next to the toilet bowl.

Now that he was in here, the stench from the 'medicines' was so overpowering he felt light-headed, not to mention still nauseous from Ma Yeasty's snot-and-spit-fest. He'd been making panicky conversation with the pharmacist just to distract himself from the urge to be sick all over the shop floor, and now he wasn't entirely sure what he'd said. Mr Brimstone was looking at him suspiciously, paused in the act of reaching for the fragrant herb jar on the shelf.

'Where's your Miss Happyday, then? She never comes in here anymore . . .'

Stef began to sweat. He wasn't any good at lying, and it was very important that they didn't get into a conversation about the matron.

'. . . her coffin,' finished the pharmacist.

Stef's head jerked up as if on a string. 'Coffin? There's no coffin. Coffins are for dead people, and no one's dead. Why would you say that?'

Mr Brimstone's face screwed up in irritation. 'What are you blathering on about? I said she doesn't come in here anymore – last time I had my best incense burning and she reckoned it gave her a coughing fit. She's got a nerve, saying that. Everyone knows inhaling any kind of smoke is good for the lungs. They have to work harder to get air in, and of course working harder makes you fitter. It's common sense. All the top doctors agree.'

'Oh! *Coughing!* I thought you said . . . No, she never coughs, because she's . . . because she's . . . so healthy and everything. There's definitely nothing wrong with Miss Happyday.' Stef tugged at his collar. All his pores had suddenly exploded with sweat, and his neck was slippery with it. *Do not talk about her being dead. She's not dead. She's not buried under the vegetable garden. Not even slightly.*

Mr Brimstone peered forward at him over the desk. 'Is she up to something? Trying to stir up some health scandal, get me into trouble? DEATH were here asking all sorts of difficult questions the other week, and that's just the kind of thing she'd be involved in. Haven't set eyes on her for a long time, but I thought I could see her hand in it. Rotten snitch.'

'You can't see her hand!' Stef blustered. 'Even though it's above ground, like the rest of her.' *Stop talking, for crying out loud.* 'And it's not rotten, either . . .'

The pharmacist leaned back again and contemplated him.

'Something funny's going on. She's been avoiding me. Or is she ill?'

Stef shuddered with relief. Finally a truth he could tell! 'No, she's not ill.'

'Eww, is that blood coming out of your nose? Great Scott! I've never seen that much—'

'Must be off now. Bye!'

The door closed behind him just as Mr Brimstone called out, 'Wait, you forgot—'

Stef didn't care. Escape from the shop was all that mattered. No bathroom pong needed fixing that badly.

Chapter Eight

Back at St Halibut's, Arfur scratched his chin, apparently deep in thought. 'Bingo! Knew it. Crossed my mind she'd been murdered, but that don't make sense – you kids wouldn't 'ave been left alive.'

'We might,' said Herc. 'It's her that wasn't very popular.'

'Trust me, neither are you lot,' said Arfur. 'Nah, I believe you. This is what you call a fluke. An unlikely throw of the dice. And the second time this week! It's this sorta thing made me give up gamblin'.'

'What are you on about?' Tig asked him, despite herself. He was being irritatingly mysterious.

But he merely jabbed her gleefully in the ribs with his elbow. 'Unless it *was* you what bumped her off, yer cheeky so-and-sos . . .'

'I was there,' insisted Herc solemnly. 'And I watched it happen, but I didn't do it. And neither did anyone else. It was the books.'

'All righty. Made the best of it, though, 'aven't you, to say the least! Ha! I knew you was up to something, but I have to admit you've surprised even me. Shocked, I am. And a little bit impressed, if I'm honest. So what's all the cleaning in aid of?'

'None of your business,' Tig replied, at exactly the same time as Herc said, 'Mr Fleetham is coming to see us and it has to be perfect!'

'Herc!' Tig's sharp tone closed her brother's mouth into a worried wobble, and a sliver of guilt pricked her. 'It's all right. Go and tidy upstairs, will you?' Instantly Herc's expression cleared, and he scampered off.

She turned back to Arfur with a sigh. It was so tiring, having to manage them all the time. Stef thought about things so much he never got around to doing them, and Herc did everything without thinking – if she didn't keep them in line, everything would fall apart. She felt like a drill sergeant, except her soldiers were Labrador puppies, and every time she turned her back they pooed on the parade ground.

Arfur was waiting expectantly, leaning against the door frame. He couldn't have looked more entertained if he'd been eating popcorn.

She thought about making something up, but what was the point? The cat was well and truly out of the bag now. 'Someone's coming from DEATH. We have an inspection to prepare for.'

'Deary, deary me, I see your problem. Not meaning to be rude, love, but they ain't gonna like what they see, are they?' He giggled. 'Looks like a bomb's gone off. And I bet the rest is worse, innit?'

'Quite. So if you don't mind . . .'

But he wasn't done yet. 'The lovely lady's been gone a while, eh? Well I never. So . . . leave anything behind, did she? You oughta search her room. I'd be happy to lend a hand. Bit of a spendthrift, your matron was. Liked a bit of bling, didn't she? You never know, she might have kept a few secrets. Trinkets and the like. Items of value.' He studied his grubby fingernails with great interest, as though wondering whether they too might be worth something.

So now they came to it.

'How much do you want?' Tig asked him coldly. 'To keep quiet?'

Arfur placed an open palm on his chest in dismay. 'I can't believe you've brought that up. What a mind, to think of money at such a time! But since you have, gotta tell you I don't rightly know. Need some time to think about your kind offer.'

'You do that.'

'It would help if I knew the kind of sum that's possible . . . I mean, if you're only sitting on a handful of coppers I might need to go elsewhere to make some money, if you get my drift.'

Ugh, how Tig hated him and every hair on his greasy head! She wondered if the oiliness was the result of some unpleasant disease. It was combed so precisely it seemed intentional, yet it was hard to imagine anyone slathering that on one morning and being pleased enough with the effect ever to do it again. Perhaps it helped him to slither his way out when he got into trouble. Certainly nothing he deserved ever stuck to the slimy little toad. It was a mystery how he was able to wander around freely, without being prosecuted for a hundred different trading standards offences. Maisie had told them that he worked for Ainderby Myers at the Mending House from time to time, though, which probably explained why he kept getting away with things. 'There's plenty of money. But you can't come in now.'

It seemed he was about to argue, but then stopped short, as though a penny had dropped somewhere in his brain. 'You know what? No need, after all. That's grand.' He beamed. 'And now we have an understanding, if there's anything else I can do to help, you only have to ask. *Anything*. Just say the word. I'm here for you.'

'How nice! Best friends for ever, yay. Can't wait to spend long evenings together, blackmailing each other. What larks.' She gestured at the broom propped up against the door frame, calling his bluff. 'If you want to help, get sweeping.'

He winced. 'Anything else. Can't do that. It's me back, see. Also, I'm allergic to dust.' This last said sadly, as though he had once dreamed of being able to sweep floors and was bravely learning to live with the disappointment. How on earth had Maisie ever liked this man enough to marry him?

'Fine. The inspector will be here on Friday. Stay away till Saturday and then we'll talk.'

'Sure you don't want my help on Friday? I could, you know, put in a good word for you kids. Make sure the inspector don't miss nothing important.'

Tig's withering stare gave Arfur the answer. She knew what kind of word he'd put in with Kirkby Fleetham. If Arfur thought he could get more money out of the inspector as a reward than he could get out of the children as blackmail, he wouldn't just tell their secret, he'd sing it like a canary.

His enthusiasm was not dampened by her expression. 'Come on. Don't be shy. You could do with a friend like me. I've skills and experience what could be to your advantage. Got me finger in plenty of pies, if you know what I mean.'

'Big deal. So does Ma Yeasty, and we all wish she didn't.'

Arfur tipped his head regretfully. 'So be it. Nice doing business with you anyway, young lady. Hope it goes well and I'll see you on Friday.' He was trotting down the steps away from her at speed.

'Saturday!' she called after him. 'And we have lots of money. *Lots!* OK?'

He turned and gave her a mock salute by way of reply.

'You stay away till Saturday, you hear!' she yelled after him. 'SATURDAY!'

But he was too far away to hear her.

Chapter Nine

'Be funny if he's late.'

Stef didn't look amused. 'Won't happen. Those people don't know *how* to be late. They're not capable of it. Like fishes trying to ride a bike.'

'So, where is he? Unless he can fly, he's not going to make it in time.'

It was Friday. The last two days had been spent cleaning so frantically their hands were red-raw, and Tig couldn't shake the feeling she'd forgotten something important, but it was too late now. They were at the edge of the drive, squinting down the hill. The low early-morning sun gilded the frosty rocks on the path with an eye-watering shine. As one, they shielded their faces against the glare.

'You're right. But I don't see anyth— Hold on, what's that right at the bottom, at the edge of the village?'

There was a pause. 'No, that's just Maisie starting the deliveries with Bernard.' Bernard was Maisie's tough little

pony, who pulled the mail cart when needed.

'Oh. Yeah.'

'The letter definitely said today, right?'

'We both checked it. You know we did.'

They scanned the hillside, listening to the stiff grass rustle. Behind them the house was silent, the very stone holding its breath. Herc was under strict orders to hide from the inspector at all times. He'd been quite up for this, since hide-and-seek was his favourite game.

'Forgot to tell you,' Stef said, just to break the tense silence. 'I found out why Miss Happyday was climbing the shelves in the library. She was high on sugar. Ma Yeasty put a load in the cake she gave to Herc, the matron ate the half he made it home with, but it sent her, well . . . up the wall.'

Tig made a mildly interested noise. 'Couldn't take it, eh?'

'Oh, and Bickley Brimstone was asking about her. Miss Happyday, I mean.'

Herc's voice came from the doorway. 'Oh, *him.* I don't like Mr Brimstone. He told me off once for playing in his shop. He said some of his powders were very powerful mixed together and that I could blow up the whole shop, and I thought he meant I should try it, so I lit one of his matches, and he threw me out.'

Tig rounded on him and hissed through gritted teeth, 'For the LAST TIME, Herc. You are HIDING. In the sense of not being seen, or heard, until I say you can come out. How was that not clear to you?'

The sound of a raspberry being blown reached them, but then Herc fell blessedly silent.

Tig exhaled slowly and closed her eyes. 'That Mr Brimstone is quite sharp,' she murmured to Stef. 'I hope you didn't let anything slip out.'

'Of course not,' Stef scoffed in an offended tone, trying very hard not to recall the conversation and any mention he might have made of dead bodies and coffins and the matron's state of health. 'I was incredibly discreet.'

A cheerful greeting made them whip round.

'Good morning!'

The person who had appeared from round the side of the house did not look as though he had just climbed a nearly vertical cliff face and then scrambled over a fence, and yet that is what he must have done, because they'd been watching the other side for an hour. He walked towards them with regular, unhurried steps: ordinary height and build, dressed neatly in a grey suit, wearing a trilby hat, carrying a small black briefcase in his left hand, looking for all the world as though he had just been dropped off by a carriage. Unless . . . he had come up earlier.

Much earlier. And been watching.

Tig's mouth hung open and Stef was clutching at her, having almost jumped into her arms. They watched, stunned, as he approached. His smile was polite, amiable.

'G-good morning,' Tig managed. 'We were . . . We didn't . . . How did you . . .' She glanced back at the path, and then craned round the visitor to the vegetable garden, as though he might have sprouted there, along with the carrots.

He inclined his head a little, waiting patiently.

'We didn't see you come up,' finished Tig, feeling as though this man had deftly removed the ground from under their feet with a single tug.

'No, indeed. You did not.' He spoke slowly, precisely, as though each of his words had been picked out and dusted off before being presented. His ID card glinted in the sun, the DEATH logo – a grinning skull – appearing to wink at them. He showed no sign of explaining further. 'I am Mr Kirkby Fleetham, as you can see. And to whom do I have the pleasure of speaking?'

Finally Tig's presence of mind returned. 'My name is Tig, and this is Stef.' She stuck out her hand. He observed it with interest and apparent amusement, and then shook it. His hand was cool, his grip neither tight nor limp.

He repeated the process with Stef, who looked moments away from throwing up.

He tipped his hat, and then leaned in conspiratorially. 'Shall we go in? I am very much looking forward to seeing your matron. She has quite the reputation.'

He turned and marched up to the front door.

'Um, about that. She's not actually here at the moment.' The calm and capable tone Tig was aiming for had sneaked off and deserted her.

Mr Fleetham's hand stopped on the doorknob. 'I beg your pardon?'

'She's had an emergency. A family thing.'

Mr Fleetham was less bothered by this than they had expected. 'I see. Well. No matter. Today I am more interested in seeing the place than interviewing her. I will return another time, perhaps in a day or two.'

'No!' Both Stef and Tig said at the same time, rather loudly.

The inspector raised an eyebrow.

'I mean,' Tig stammered. 'She could be . . . she could be gone for ages. She sends her apologies.'

'Come, come. You are not suggesting that Miss Happyday would abandon you for long? DEATH would be *most* concerned to hear that.'

Stef leaped in. 'Course not. She'll be back before you

leave.' He ignored Tig's look of incredulous dismay as she silently mouthed, *What?* 'Till then, we can show you around.'

The inspector nodded. 'I do indeed intend to see every nook and cranny of this house. However, I do not need an escort. You may simply furnish me with any appropriate keys, and I will let you know if you are needed.'

Tig swallowed the panic that threatened to rise in her throat. There was no way he was getting the key to Miss Happyday's room. 'But . . . that will take a long time. You must have a Schedule to keep to.'

Mr Fleetham stared at her blankly. 'My dear child, you have it all wrong. I am a senior employee of the most important and powerful government department in the land. I do not keep to the Schedule. The Schedule keeps to me.'

And with that, he turned the doorknob.

On the threshold he paused, and turned to the horrified children. 'Don't look so miserable. This is going to be fun.'

Stef and Tig exchanged glances. There were 2,000 volumes of *The Rules and Philosophy of DEATH,* and the word 'fun' did not feature in any of them.

This was the first clue that the day was not going to run quite as expected.

Unfortunately, the second clue was that one end of

the lintel over the door chose that moment to come loose from Stef's hastily hammered-in nail. It seemed to swing downwards in slow motion, but there was no mistaking the force with which it met the side of Mr Fleetham's skull.

There was the sickening thud of wood on flesh and bone, and then a polite rustle as the inspector sank gracefully to the floor.

Stef and Tig were bent over the fallen man and failed to notice that Herc had popped his head out of the front door.

'Is he going to be inspecting everything that closely?' he asked, perplexed. 'His nose is squished right up against the ground.'

'Get back inside,' hissed Tig. She should have known he wouldn't be able to stay still for long. She'd hoped he might do what he was told for an hour or two, but it turned out that his limit was less than two minutes.

Stef held the back of his hand against Mr Fleetham's mouth. 'He's breathing. I think he's just unconscious. He might wake up at any time.'

'You were supposed to fix that lintel!'

'I did. It just broke again – I was in a hurry. You should have done it.'

'Me? I can't do *everything*.' She clutched at her hair. 'This is terrible. We're supposed to be making an impression.'

'We definitely have,' said Stef, contemplating Mr Fleetham's wound.

'We can't let him think it's our fault. And what on

earth were you thinking, telling him Miss Happyday will be here later?'

'Don't worry, I've got an idea. If he sees her, he won't need to come back, will he?'

'Stef, you can't be ser—'

As she spoke, Mr Fleetham stirred slightly, and groaned. Tig gestured frantically at Herc to go back into the house and hide. He gave her the world's largest eye-roll and sloped off.

'W-what happened?' The inspector pulled himself to sit up a little.

'You fainted,' said Tig firmly. 'That's quite a bruise you're going to have. I think you should go home and rest. Probably seen enough here anyway, haven't you?' she suggested hopefully.

He touched a finger to his wound and winced. 'Something hit me.'

'Hit you? Nope. You're imagining it. Isn't he?' Tig said, appealing to Stef.

Stef was holding up the lintel above his head in its rightful place, while attempting to stand casually. 'Yes. What could have hit you around here, anyway?'

Mr Fleetham was contemplating the sky warily, as though expecting a shower of heavy objects to come raining down on him.

Tig helped him gently to his feet. He now had a rapidly swelling bump on his temple.

'You hit your head when you fell. You probably have concussion,' she said firmly. 'Tell you what, we won't mind if you just pop off down the hill again, will we, Stef?'

Stef was currently incapable of further speech, straining with the effort of nonchalantly holding his weight in wooden beam above his head.

Mr Fleetham shook his head, then appeared to regret that. 'No, no, I must . . . complete my inspection. First, perhaps a cup of tea to help me regain my strength? Ah, this young man can get it for me.' To Tig's horror, Herc had appeared back at the door like a jack-in-the-box whose lid has broken. 'Peppermint tea, boy. With honey, if you have it. Make it strong.'

It was clear this man was going nowhere.

'All right,' came Stef's somewhat strained voice. 'Herc, go . . . ungh . . . and make him a nice cup . . . aargh . . . of tea.'

'But where—' started Herc.

'Chop chop . . .' gasped Stef. Herc shrugged and went back in. There was nothing else to be done. Tig helped Mr Fleetham over the doorstep into the house.

It had been a terrible start to the inspection.

At least, she consoled herself, it couldn't get any worse.

Chapter Ten

'Guv? Guv?' The unwelcome noise of one of the guards – Buttly, or possibly Donk, or Jerkson, he could never tell them apart – landed in Myers' ear like a persistent fly. It was the last thing he wanted to hear when he was enjoying his meal at one end of the empty dining hall, trying to finish it in peace before the arrival of the revolting Mended children spoilt his appetite. The man was carrying a huge saucepan full of gruel.

Myers hated the way his henchmen called him 'Guv', as though he were some grubby foreman on a building site. Usually this one was on the gates, along with another guard or two, striking muscular poses for the benefit of passers-by. All his thugs, apart from Snepp, were lazy lunkheads, who worked out the minimum effort they could put in to achieve something, then halved it. It was so hard to find good staff, and they always disappointed

him. It was like thinking you were buying pedigree guard dogs but realizing when you come to train them that they're actually just a pile of odd socks that smell like wet fur. But unfortunately, Myers could not supervise every corner of his domain at once.

'Guv, I done the gruel.'

'I can see that, Buttly.'

'I'm Jerkson, Guv. So . . . what do I do now?'

Myers' fists twitched. 'For pity's sake! What do you always do at this time of day? You bring them in and feed them.'

Jerkson's gaze travelled along the benches in doubtful awe, as if he'd just been asked to scale Everest. 'What, all of 'em? Again? I did it yesterday.'

Myers let his stare rest gently on Jerkson's eyeballs like a red-hot poker. Jerkson blinked, and then went to get the Mended.

The Guvnor's mood did not improve when Arfur was escorted in to see him.

Every now and then, Ainderby Myers considered disposing of Arfur. He would enjoy doing it, and it would remove one of the fears that kept him awake at night. But it would create problems too, because unfortunately Arfur was necessary.

Arfur's knowledge was valuable. He knew who lived

where, how rich they were, what treasures they had in their houses, and when they would be out. He knew how many servants were in every mansion in Lardidar Valley, and how much they needed to be bribed to leave a window open, just a crack. He knew which guard dogs would roll over for a morsel of chicken, and which would tear you to pieces instead. He'd tested that, once, and Arfur had been right – it had been a terrible waste of a Mended burglar. Since Myers would not leave the Mending House, the con man was essential to his burglary operations. Which made it all the more galling that he thought he could just turn up whenever he liked. His visits had been less and less frequent lately, as if he had better things to do.

'Is that all?' Myers said quietly, once he had absorbed Arfur's information. The Mended were now filing silently in, sinking to the benches and picking up their spoons.

Arfur shrugged infuriatingly. 'Just thought you'd want to know – who's on their 'olidays, who's been jewellery shopping. So here I am.'

'Lucky me.' The sarcasm dripped so heavily off the Guvnor's words that Arfur looked down at his shoes, half expecting them to be standing in a puddle of it.

'Look. Just helping you out . . . for old times' sake, all right?'

A sour laugh bubbled up from inside Myers. 'Oh, yes, we're friends, aren't we?'

Arfur actually flushed. 'Come on, now. By the way, had any trouble from them matrons lately?'

Myers turned to him sharply. 'Why? What have they said to you?'

'Nothing, nothing. Only I know what moaning minnies they are. You should teach 'em a lesson.'

'They'll get what's coming to them, don't you worry. As will you, if you don't stay out of my business. Sometimes I think you've forgotten what I did for you, *thief*.'

Myers found he had shouted the last word, his face quivering with rage half an inch from Arfur. He checked his tone. Although the guards struggled to take an interest in anything that couldn't be eaten or punched, there was no need for Myers to broadcast his personal business.

The Mended shouldn't care what was being said, either, but he was a cautious man. They were sitting silently at the benches now, eating their gruel – just enough to keep them alive, without causing him too much expense. It constantly amazed him how quickly a lack of food and a smattering of cruel words could make them lose hope. After a few special talks from him, a few repeated phrases, their eyes would glaze over, and they found it easiest just to obey and believe whatever they were told. After that, the work, the routine, the general atmosphere of hopelessness and despair – all finished the job of Mending. He had found that, after a while, they all Mended each other, like spreading a disease.

'I do know . . .' Arfur began. 'I owe you . . . my life.'

'Correct. So don't try to give me advice, as if you're cleverer than me.' He flicked a coin on to the ground and watched as Arfur hesitated, then awkwardly bent to pick it up.

Through the window, he watched Arfur departing from the gates and despised him more than ever.

He failed to notice the Mended child whose eyes were not downcast like the others, but watching.

Chapter Eleven

Mr Fleetham appeared to be feeling slightly better; he and Tig were sitting together in the kitchen while he sipped his tea. Stef had taken Herc off with him somewhere 'on an errand' – presumably to keep him away from the inspector. The conversation wasn't exactly flowing – she'd asked him three times if the tea was OK, if it had enough honey in it – but at least she was making him comfortable. It would all help for his report.

His hand as he held his cup was steady, even though he winced in pain from time to time. Perhaps there would be no long-term damage.

At least, not to him. But if they didn't pull off a miracle somehow, there would most certainly be to them.

For a split second when Stef opened the door and made his announcement, Tig wondered if there had actually been such a miracle, even if it was of the terrifying and unnatural kind.

'Miss Happyday will see you now,' he said. 'She's back.'

Tig tried to play it cool, and failed. 'Hahahawhat?'

'Very well,' said Mr Fleetham, rising a little too fast and grabbing hold of a chair to keep his balance. 'Ooh! Whoops.'

'Watch your step, Inspector,' said Tig. 'You a bit dizzy?'

'No, no, I'm fine,' he said, brushing her off.

Stef led them to the ground-floor study, and stopped in front of the closed door.

'Now,' he said. 'She's not feeling very well, I'm afraid. She has a headache. So the curtains are shut, to make it nice and dark.'

Mr Fleetham nodded. 'Yes, yes. I'm feeling rather nauseous myself. I shan't keep her long.'

Stef licked his lips. 'And . . . she's got a temperature, so she's wrapped up warm. Lots of layers.'

The inspector waved him away from the door. 'I don't care about that.'

'And . . . she, um, has a sore throat. So don't ask her anything.'

Tig started to get a very bad feeling about this.

'Good grief, you are very tiresome. I have an inspection to do, boy.'

Stef reluctantly moved aside and opened the door.

With a sigh of impatience Mr Fleetham entered the study. Over his shoulder, Tig could dimly make out some shapes.

There, in the corner, sat Herc. And next to him on the low couch was another person, dressed in what appeared to be every item from Miss Happyday's wardrobe, including a large flowered hat pulled down low over her face. Herc was cuddling up to her.

'Miss Happyday?' asked Mr Fleetham, peering into the darkness.

There was a soft bleat from the pile of clothes.

Uh-oh.

Herc patted the skirts reassuringly.

'Madam, I shall be having a look around St Halibut's today,' said Mr Fleetham, 'but there is no need to trouble yourself to get up. I will return on another occasion to speak to you.' Even in the dark, Tig could see the inspector was perspiring heavily, beads of moisture glimmering on his eyebrows. Perhaps he had a temperature himself. He took off his hat and wiped his forehead, showering drops of sweat.

'No!' said Stef. 'Don't come back! I mean, say what you need to say now. She might . . . she might be even more sick next time.'

Tig jabbed him in the ribs. There was no doubt in her mind that the only thing stopping their goat from going on a murderous rampage right now was Herc's calming hand on her skirt.

'Don't be ridicul— Urghh.' Mr Fleetham clutched his stomach. His face was a nasty yellowish-grey colour under an oily sheen of perspiration. 'Where's the toilet? I think I'm going to—'

Luckily, one of Miss Happyday's last actions had been to install a brand-new flushing toilet downstairs, to save her having to go upstairs to her en-suite. The inspector barged Tig out of the way and staggered in the direction she indicated across the entrance hall. From behind the closed door came the sound of the contents of Mr Fleetham's stomach being forcefully ejected into the toilet bowl.

Herc called after him, 'Don't forget to flush!'

Tig rounded on Stef. 'You pillock! What were you thinking!'

He shrugged. 'What else was I supposed to do? It might work. He's a bit out of it – if he notices anything, maybe he'll think he's hallucinating, like Miss Happyday.'

'If he *notices* anything? Like the fact she's covered in white hair and has a beard and horns? Herc, get her out of here, quick. We'll say she had to go for a lie-down.'

The noises from the toilet continued as Herc hastily led Pamela out the front door, undressing her as they went. There was silence for a while and the toilet door handle began to turn, only for it to spring back and the retching noises to begin again. Tig found it hard to believe there could possibly be anything left inside the inspector to come up. 'Go and make him another cup of peppermint tea,' she told Stef. 'We've got to look after him, or he'll skewer us in his report.'

She cursed their luck. Why did he have to be ill during the inspection? He was hardly going to feel warmly towards the place after this.

He was still in the toilet two minutes later when Stef

returned, looking like he'd seen a ghost.

'Um, Tig, we have a problem.'

'Well, duh.'

'No, this one's a corker. Herc didn't use the mint tea in the kitchen for Mr Fleetham's drink; he picked the mint from that half-dead plant outside. And he got them mixed up with other things too. Half of it is lily-of-the-valley.'

She couldn't blame Herc for not getting it quite right. *The Big DEATH Book of Plants* was long buried. 'Is that bad?'

He glanced worriedly towards the toilet door. 'It's very poisonous. It's good that he's throwing it up, at least. But . . . best-case scenario is he feels terrible for a few days.'

Tig wasn't sure she wanted to ask, but did anyway. 'And the worst case?'

Stef bit his lip. 'Let's just say he'll get to spend some time with the real Miss Happyday after all.'

At that moment the toilet door finally creaked open and Mr Fleetham shuffled slowly out, bent over, as though everything hurt. His bruise was a startling combination of purple and green, in contrast to the rest of his face, which at best was a sort of light grey. At least, she thought, he must have got the worst of the poison out of his system.

'Better?' asked Tig brightly. 'You'll be wanting to get off home now, I expect.'

Mr Fleetham lifted his head, and his grimace made her shudder. A long line of drool twisted gently to the floor from his rubbery lip.

'It takes more than a bit of sickness to stop me,' he said. 'I'm not leaving till I've found—' He broke off. 'I have a job to do. And I'm not leaving until I've done it.'

Tig swallowed.

'But I am . . .' he said, 'I find I am rather fatigued. Perhaps to save time . . . I might be shown . . . certain places, after all.'

Tig suppressed a huge grin. 'Absolutely. Come with me. I can answer all your questions.'

'Not you.' Mr Fleetham narrowed his eyes and lifted a trembling finger to point over her shoulder to the front door, where Herc had just come back from settling Pamela in her shed. 'Him.'

Chapter Twelve

Kirkby Fleetham had not, in fact, flushed the toilet, as Herc pointed out to him crossly. Herc was frequently told off for such things himself, and berated the inspector with the zeal of the very newly converted. But the inspector had other things on his mind.

'Now,' Mr Fleetham whispered in Herc's ear. He smelt of sick. 'I bet a house like this is good to play hide-and-seek in. Lots of nooks and crannies.'

Herc knew the answer to this one. 'We don't play hide-and-seek.'

Mr Fleetham smiled, and wiped his damp brow. 'Of course. It is not on the curriculum. I can see you are a very clever boy.'

Herc shrugged; this was undoubtedly true. 'I like your badge. The skull is good.' He liked the way the hollow eyes followed him when the card moved.

'It's nice, isn't it? Let me put this another way. I

inspect things and my job is to inspect the parts of this house that are . . . secret. The places Miss Happyday does not like you to go, the ones perhaps she has told you not to show me. A clever boy like you must know about all the most interesting things in the house.'

Herc examined his feet, Tig's instructions ringing in his ears. It was very tempting to show Mr Fleetham his store of powders from the pharmacist, which he had been experimenting with. He reckoned he could make fireworks with the right combination, though so far he had only succeeded in burning a hole through the attic floor. But he was pretty sure that was exactly the sort of thing Tig would prefer to be kept hidden. There were other possibilities, however, now he thought about it, if it was *interesting* things that the inspector wanted.

Mr Fleetham smiled again. 'I promise you won't get into trouble. But those are the very places I must see. And then I can go back to DEATH and tell them everything is in order. Tell you what: show me, and you can hold my badge for a minute.' He took it from around his neck and placed it round Herc's.

Herc considered this. 'And the hat?'

A flash of irritation passed over the inspector's face. But then he removed the hat and placed it on Herc's head, where it slipped over his eyes.

When Herc pulled up the brim, his expression was solemn.

'Inspector, what I am about to show you has never before been shown to anyone outside St Halibut's.' He lowered his voice. 'It is *top* secret, and you won't be able to believe your eyes. So you must guard this knowledge with your life.'

Mr Fleetham looked as excited as a puppy who has just been told he's going for walkies off the lead in a sausage factory. 'Oh, very much so.'

Herc went for it. 'And I get to keep these for ever.'

Mr Fleetham grinned widely. 'I promise that if you show me, I won't be needing them back.'

Herc nodded casually, like one who is completely cool about having just gained a *hat* and a *badge* for a couple of minutes' work. 'Come with me.'

The inspector seemed hesitant when Herc showed him the secret place.

'In the garden? Are you sure? I don't see anything.'

Herc felt almost dizzy with the heady power that he possessed. The temptation to stretch out the moment was irresistible.

'It's not *in* the garden, it's *under* the garden.' He waggled his eyebrows knowledgeably. In the corner of

his vision he saw his sister's and Stef's faces watching through the kitchen window, frozen in dread. Suckers. If they'd wanted the hat and badge for themselves, they shouldn't have been so chicken.

'Something . . . buried?' said the inspector, jerking to attention. 'Treasure?'

'Sort of,' Herc said, flicking a catch with his foot. An access grille dropped open next to them and he swept his arms towards it like a magician revealing a rabbit.

The stench hit them like a steam train.

'SWEET HOLY MACKEREL!' Fleetham's hands flew to his face. 'WHAT THE BLAZES . . . FOR THE LOVE OF—'

Herc stood by politely while the inspector ran through a range of expressions of surprise. It was to be expected – grown-ups were kind of pathetic. They couldn't handle sugar, and they had very sensitive nostrils.

'Trust me. This is *brilliant*,' Herc insisted. 'The others are always telling me not to go down here. In fact, when I suggested I take you there today they totally freaked out.'

He dropped down through the hole, leaving Mr Fleetham peering after him into the gloom.

'Urgh! What's down there?' the inspector called, muffled through his fingers.

'A ledge. Come on, I'm standing on it. You can fit too, but be careful because it's quite narrow. You've got to see what's here. They'll *kill* me for bringing you, but it's worth it.'

Mr Fleetham glanced around, unsure. He caught sight of the two panicked faces at the window. That seemed to decide him. Gingerly he lowered himself down, and immediately gagged, grabbing on to Herc for balance. 'This is—'

'An underground lake of poo!' said Herc proudly. He had always wondered where everything went after it had gone down the toilet, and had been fascinated to discover this place a few months ago. To be able to share it with someone was exhilarating. 'Let's see if we can spot what you did earlier. It was sort of yellowy, wasn't it? Some of the lumps might be floating.'

There was silence. The inspector was probably already planning what glowing phrases to write in his report. It was a fair bet that, in all his years of inspecting, he'd never seen anything quite like this before.

'Mr Fleetham?'

There was a movement in the air beside Herc, and then a large splash.

Chapter Thirteen

It was a beautiful, if chilly day as Stef, Tig and Herc stood on the grass considering their options. In a few weeks, the delicate scent of daffodils would be carried on the breeze, along with other pleasing aromas of spring. Birdsong would fill the air. It would be warm enough to sit on the wooden bench at the side of the house and take in the view of the wide stretch of grass, the new life surging from the vegetable garden.

For now, the view and the air were somewhat spoilt by the body of Mr Fleetham, DEATH inspector, now dead inspector.

It had taken some time to fish him out of the cesspit, as he kept slipping off the long branches they were using to hook into his trousers. By the time he was lying on the grass, they were all sweating and out of breath.

Herc had explained exactly what had happened, acting out the entire scene, taking Mr Fleetham's part, and ending by clutching his chest and falling convincingly to the floor. Then he got to his feet, suddenly worried. 'It wasn't my fault, was it?' he asked. 'Did I do it? Am I a murderer?'

'Of course not. Sounds like he had a heart attack,' Tig said quickly. 'Nothing to do with you. Would have happened anyway. Just bad luck. Although,' she said slowly, 'maybe not so bad after all.'

Stef glanced sharply at her. 'What?'

'Well.' She shrugged. 'Looks like our, er, difficulty has gone away.'

Stef was regarding her with something like horror. Herc had already lost interest in the conversation and began running a looping figure of eight around the grass.

'I mean, obviously it's very sad,' she said quickly. 'Tragic. May he rest in ashes, pieces, dust, whatever, amen. All that. But, y'know . . . problem solved.'

Stef frowned, disapproval radiating from his lowered brow. Mr Fleetham might have had a family – children, maybe a little dog. He felt his eyes beginning to sting with tears at the thought of a loyal, waggy-tailed spaniel eagerly awaiting his master's return – a master who would never come home, because he had drowned in sewage. Stef sometimes wondered whether Tig had a heart at all.

He sniffed, and busied himself with the catches on Mr

Fleetham's briefcase, which they had also fished out. The briefcase popped open, and he picked up the top sheet from the papers within, clearing the lump from his throat. 'This is his schedule. Looks like he was due at St Cod's after us, at two o'clock. Then he has to report back by six o'clock.'

'Well,' said Tig cheerfully, 'he won't be giving DEATH a bad report about us, that's for sure. Oh . . .' At once her face drained of colour, 'he won't be giving them any report. And at six o'clock . . .' She trailed off.

Stef understood her meaning immediately. '. . . they'll know something's up.'

'And they'll come looking for him.'

Stef groaned softly.

'Stop that,' Tig snapped at him. 'Get a grip. Think. *Think!*'

'I don't know!' he wailed. 'What are we going to do?'

Tig was staring intently at the body as if the answer lay there. 'Let's be logical. DEATH don't get the report. What will they do?'

'They'll go asking at the last place he was supposed to be seen, and then if he's not there, the place before that.'

'You're right. Ugh. Why couldn't he have waited till he was at St Cod's to die? That would have been perfect. If anyone needs an inspection, it's them.' A thought revealed itself to Tig with such a jolt she gasped. 'What if he did?'

'Who? Did what?'

'Inspect them. What if Mr Fleetham *could* inspect St Cod's? Then they wouldn't even search here.'

He looked at her incredulously for a moment. 'Let's ask him, shall we?' He bent down to the inspector's ear and shouted into it. 'Mr Fleetham, are you up for some more inspecting? Only, we were hoping you could pop down the hill and ask the St Cod's folks a few questions before we tuck you up in your grave. That OK?' He cupped his ear to the corpse. 'What's that you say?' He nodded, concentrating. 'OK, I'll tell her. Sorry, Tig, he says he can't because he's busy BEING DEAD.' His voice had risen a couple of octaves, verging on hysterical.

'Obviously *he* can't. But *someone* could.' She pointed at the schedule impatiently. 'If someone turns up at St Cod's at two o'clock today and says they're a DEATH inspector, how's anyone to know different? St Cod's will be expecting one.'

It was a ridiculous suggestion. But then ridiculous was fast becoming their speciality. 'Well . . . who's going to do that for us?'

'Me!' yelled Herc, who had reappeared between them without either of them noticing. Tig patted her chest, reassuring her poor stuttering heart. She really needed to have a word with him about jumping out at them like that. It must be taking years off her life.

'This is serious, Herc.'

'I don't think Pamela's the right person for the job this time,' reflected Stef.

'She wasn't the right person for it last time, either.'

'Me! Please, please!' Herc had grabbed Tig's shirt and was tugging it up and down as he bounced on the spot.

She chewed on her nail thoughtfully. 'I wondered about Maisie, but it's too risky to tell another person. Besides, everyone knows her too well. No, it needs to be one of us. Someone who can pass as an adult.' She raised her eyes slowly to meet Stef's.

There was a long silence. Understanding crept over Stef's face like the light of dawn – the kind of dawn that means the sun is exploding and the world is on fire.

'No way.' He shook his head vigorously. 'I'm no good at that sort of thing.'

'Come on. All you'd have to do is stand there and ask a couple of questions, then leave. Even you can do that.'

It did not escape Stef's notice that, even when trying to persuade him, she managed to insult him.

'Why can't *you* do it, if it's such a good idea?'

'I'd never pass as an adult.' It was undeniable. Tig was

slight of frame, and short. She looked more like ten than the twelve years she actually was. 'It has to be you.'

'Let me do it!' said Herc. 'I want to be the inspector. I'd be brilliant. Listen: *I am here to test you on your spellings!*' he purred, doing a fair impression of Mr Fleetham.

Tig ignored him. 'Stef, it's got to be you.' Herc kicked her shin.

Stef backed off from the pair of them, hands up as though warding off blows. 'Can you even hear me? No way. You've lost your mind. You know what they say about the matron down there, Miss Lackspittle. She's a giant and she eats children. *Eats* them.'

'Come on, you don't really believe that, do you?' snorted Tig. 'You're too big for fairy tales.' She was considering him thoughtfully, her head on one side. 'I suppose with a moustache or something . . . And if you could stop picking your nose for five minutes.'

'A moust— Have you listened to anything I just said? I am not going down to St Cod's, I am not inspecting anything, and I am not pretending to be *him*. You know what they're like down there. Even if Miss Lackspittle didn't kill me, the orphans would.'

'They wouldn't,' said Tig, choosing to believe fully in the one per cent chance he was wrong. 'They're just petty thieves. Nobody would kill a DEATH inspector.' She paused, then conceded, 'Except us, obviously.'

Stef drew himself up to his full height and crossed his arms over his chest. He was a lot bigger than Tig, and it was time to stop letting her push him around.

'Nope. Never going to happen. I'm sorry, but there it is.'

There. Finally he'd stood up to her properly.

It felt good.

Chapter Fourteen

Stef had an overwhelming urge to turn and run from the heavy wooden door whose knocker he had just flicked gently, with one finger. He had tried to touch the thing enough to say he'd definitely knocked it, but not so much that anyone inside might actually hear it. He reckoned if he waited ten seconds it would mean no one was in. Five seconds was plenty, come to think of it.

His upper lip tickled, unused to the goat-hair moustache he was wearing, stuck on with honey. His chin was only slightly less itchy, now that he had removed the stray stems of hay from his new beard. Herc had been rather hasty in gathering Pamela's moulted hairs from her stall and, so far, as well as the hay, Stef had picked out several insects, a daisy and a small foul-smelling brown pellet that he had decided to believe was a squashed berry of some kind. He had to breathe through his mouth,

since he had small wads of cotton stuffed up his nose to stem the nosebleed that was surely inevitable as soon as he started speaking the first untruth. It wasn't as though he *wanted* to lie. It was necessary. But his body wouldn't listen to excuses – a lie was a lie, and it would be marked by a gush of blood as his capillaries popped in disgust. He was also starting to feel a horribly familiar rolling and churning in his stomach.

He'd made quite an exhibition of himself on the way through town to St Cod's. Tig had been firm that people had to see him visiting. There had to be witnesses, in order that when DEATH came looking, anyone who happened to be around could say they'd seen Mr Fleetham, and yes, he'd definitely been at St Cod's that afternoon. And so Stef had hummed tunelessly as he walked, raised Mr Fleetham's thankfully unsoiled hat, shouted 'Good day!' gruffly to shopkeepers and passers-by, and polished the ID card with a handkerchief while loudly declaring that it was so important to keep one's DEATH credentials clean and shiny. Most people, as a result, had scattered out of his path. Which was fine. It meant the disguise was working, at least from a distance.

St Cod's itself felt unnerving, surrounded by an air of neglect. No one had cleaned the windows in years, and it was impossible to make out anything inside. It would have been easier to see through the bricks. There was an ominous silence beyond the door, a gaping, hungry emptiness that seemed to suck in the ordinary sounds of the street and suffocate them. But it wasn't only that. The Mending House was too close for comfort here: right next door, with only a narrow alley separating the two buildings, it had windows overlooking this very spot. For all he knew, Ainderby Myers might be watching him at this very moment.

Stef tried to control his ragged breathing. His nose felt like it was bulging, blood vessels swollen with the big lie of him simply standing there. He feared that the moment he spoke, it would erupt like a volcano, shooting the wads of cotton from his nostrils like red-hot boulders. Combined with the increasing chance of vomit at any moment, if anyone actually answered the door they might well get a spectacular greeting.

He heard footsteps approaching. Every cell in his body told him to get away, but his legs were frozen as an awful sense of foreboding took him over. This wasn't going to work.

Then there was a click and the door opened.

Before him stood Miss Lackspittle; she was everything he'd heard about, and more.

She was tall, and wide, in a way that suggested she

was capable of swallowing entire children like a snake. Despite the girth of her body, her head was oddly small and sharp-looking, the cheekbones protruding over hollow cheeks. She was wrapped up against the cold in a heavy cloak and scarf and what looked like several layers underneath, which gave her a lumpy appearance. Overall she had the appearance of a monstrous, badly stuffed toy with the wrong head on. A short wooden stick protruded from her mouth, and it bobbed from one side to the other as she sucked furiously on it. Her eyes travelled up and down Stef in such a disgusted and aggressive fashion that he found himself running his hands quickly over his shirt and trousers to check they were still there, and that he hadn't somehow arrived naked.

'I . . . I . . .' he stuttered.

'What d'you want?' spat Miss Lackspittle, the words muffled by the stick.

At that moment Stef remembered that the lives of three people, including his, depended on his performance. He drew in a breath. 'I am Mr Fleetham, from DEATH. You are expecting me?' He fumbled inside his shirt where the inspector's identification was hanging, and flashed it at Miss Lackspittle so quickly that she blinked and missed it. He dredged up his most outraged expression. 'Is that a *sweet* in your mouth?'

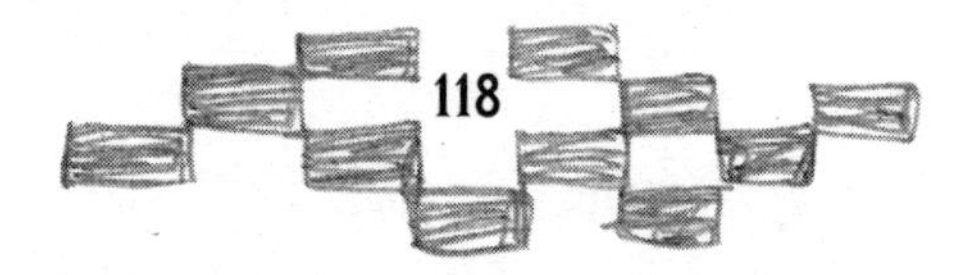

For an instant, Miss Lackspittle's face registered shock. Then an arm shot out from the depths of her cloak and yanked the lollipop from her lips with a speed that seemed to surprise even her. 'No,' she said, holding it behind her back. 'A Brussels sprout. On a stick. Only healthy treats here. You're that inspector, then. You're late. Thought you weren't coming.'

Stef puffed up his chest, trying to inhale some confidence. 'I trust you are prepared for my visit?' he boomed, his breath raising one end of his moustache. He hastily pressed it back against his upper lip.

The matron sniffed, and Stef recoiled, remembering the rumours, wondering if he smelt tasty. But she answered, 'Don't see why we need inspecting all of a sudden. Think I don't know how to run my own Home now?' As she spoke she flinched as if in pain, and staggered slightly.

'Is there something wrong?'

'Just the usual pain in the neck,' she said with a vicious glare at Stef, as though he were the pain in question. 'S'pose you'd better come in. Welcome.' She gave the word all the warmth of a bucket of ice over his head.

She led him into the drawing room with a strange lurching gait that saw her ducking at the last minute to avoid the door frame and half falling into a bookshelf before righting herself and teetering over to a wall, where she stood, steadying herself, as though she were about to collapse.

'Are you quite well?' asked Stef, alarmed. If one more person popped their clogs around him he was going to take it personally.

'I'm old,' Miss Lackspittle snapped. 'It's me bones. You inspecting me or the Home, anyhow? Get on with it, why don't you?'

She was very peculiar. Her bizarre movements made him think of a zombie. He half expected bits to start falling off her, that she'd chase him around, wielding her own body parts as weapons. He wasn't sure if that would be better or worse than her being a cannibal.

He could feel his finger aiming for the comfort of his nose like a rabbit into its burrow, and grasped it in his other hand to stop it. The room was dingy and perishingly cold. The fireplace lay black and empty, as though no fire had been lit for quite some time. No wonder the matron was wearing so many layers. He began to look at his surroundings in a manner that he hoped might pass for professional and inspectorish.

The house was clean and tidy, though that was largely due to the fact that there was almost nothing in it. Whereas St Halibut's was full of sumptuous furnishings, antique rugs and oil paintings that Miss Happyday said were essential for a grand house, the drawing room of St Cod's consisted of bare floorboards and nothing else. In fact, even some of the floorboards were missing. There were no chairs to sit on. Well, that was fine. He wasn't going to stay long enough to need a sit-down.

'Right. Let's get started, shall we?' he said. 'I will need to test the children on a few spellings, to begin with.' Although he was starting to think maybe one spelling would be enough. Then he could go. There was something decidedly odd about this place.

'No can do.'

'I beg your pardon?'

She indicated the ceiling. 'They're upstairs.'

'Well, can you call them down, please? One will be enough.'

'Nope.'

He had not expected this. She ought to be on her best behaviour, if she was truly taken in by his disguise. He patted his moustache for reassurance. 'My dear woman,' he said in what he hoped was an authoritative, patronizing tone. 'I must see the children.'

'They're sick,' she snapped back. 'And not to be disturbed.'

Stef had less expertise in lying than almost anyone in the world, but even he could tell this was a big hairy whopper. The rumours about Miss Lackspittle were crowding to the front of his mind. Despite the chill, he found he was sweating. Beads of it prickled under Pamela's hairs on his lip.

The lie sat between them, filling the entire room, daring him to point it out.

'Righto,' he said, focusing on a spot on the ceiling. Could it be that she had run out of children to consume? He didn't much like the way she was sizing him up.

'Come from St Halibut's, have you?' she asked suddenly.

'What?' His heart stuttered and then beat so fast it felt like it was running in circles around his chest, hunting for the exit. The woman had guessed, already. The game was up.

She sighed with impatience. 'Did you inspect them before us? Only I saw you come down the hill from there.'

'Oh, yes . . . yes . . . I inspected St Halibut's first.' He breathed out slowly through his mouth in order to disturb his nose as little as possible.

Miss Lackspittle grunted. 'Hmmf. Bet they were no good, were they? They need Mending, that lot. I could tell you a few things about those kids. Make your hair stand on end.'

Stef swallowed. 'That . . . won't be necessary, thank you.'

'Thieves, they are. And liars. Hoity toity. Giving us the evil eye all the time like looks could kill . . .'

'Kill?' He laughed nervously. 'I saw no evidence that they . . . that they had killed anyone. Not even accidentally,' he added, 'which would be understandable, because most accidents happen in the home, and sometimes, for example, just randomly, people get crushed by falling things, drink things they shouldn't, bang their heads, have heart attacks—' His mouth finally agreed to shut and he took a breath. 'So I just need a quick look around the house.'

There was a scuffling as Miss Lackspittle immediately lurched to block the door that presumably led upstairs.

OK. That was quite suspicious. But whatever she was trying to hide, he didn't care anymore. He was getting out of here, right now.

'I shall begin downstairs,' he told her, and backed out of the door he'd come in.

In the entrance hall, the front door stood invitingly, the only thing between him and safety. He pulled it open, sweaty hands struggling for purchase on the knob, and walked through . . . into a kitchen. In his agitation, he had walked the wrong way. He turned around, trying to get his bearings.

The kitchen was empty. There were no pots and pans,

none of the paraphernalia that cluttered the St Halibut's kitchen. Another door on the other side of the room stood ajar, and he pushed it open. The larder. Empty shelf after empty shelf. Not a single packet or pot. No cheese, or meat, or even an onion. It was as if they weren't eating anything at all. Then he saw it.

A knife. A big one. It lay on the wooden counter. Now that he was paying attention, he noticed that both the knife and the counter were stained red. Slowly, as though his body did not agree with the decision to inspect any further, he turned his head. There were red fingerprints elsewhere in the kitchen. On the cupboards. The door handle. As though there had been a struggle. Gingerly, he touched the counter stain. Wet.

There could be no doubt.

It was fresh blood.

Chapter Fifteen

Stef had been gone less than thirty minutes when Tig saw an unwelcome figure on the driveway. She had been too worried to do much more than stare into the distance, biting her nails. Suddenly she was very aware of the corpse lying on the grass. 'Quick!' she hissed at Herc. 'It's Arfur! Hide the body!'

She shrugged off her jacket and flung it over Mr Fleetham's head in one smooth movement, and the two of them formed a hasty line in front of the inspector, which might have been effective had there been twice as many of them and half as much of Mr Fleetham.

Arfur stopped in front of them and craned his neck round. 'Just came up to see how the inspector was gettin' on, but I see he's already departed.' He guffawed and slapped his thigh. 'Geddit? Departed! Aw, come on, what's with all the long faces? Cheer up, nobody died. Oops, they did – my mistake. Ha ha ha!'

They waited for him to stop sniggering.

'So . . . the inspection went well, I see.'

There seemed little point in denying it. With a sigh, Tig moved aside. 'Just go away, OK? You didn't see this. Or are you going to run down there and tell your boss?'

'Myers? The Guvnor ain't *my* guvnor. I already checked and he don't know nuffink about your matron bein' dead. Coulda told him if I wanted, couldn't I? But I didn't.' Arfur walked round behind them and prodded the partially covered figure with his boot. 'What you done to this one, eh? Come on, you can tell old Arfur.'

'Nothing,' Tig snapped. 'And don't touch him. It's disrespectful.'

He leaned in and lowered his voice conspiratorially. 'Been at your old tricks again? Now, you know I don't like to criticize, but . . . first Miss Happyday, and now . . . whatever his name is. Someone's got to say it: this is getting to be a habit.'

'No it isn't!' said Tig, through gritted teeth.

Arfur mimed exaggerated terror. 'Don't hurt me, miss, I'm too young to die!'

Herc spoke up helpfully. 'She's telling the truth. It was an accident. It's nobody's fault. Especially not mine,' he added with emphasis. 'He fell in there.' He pointed to the still-open hatch in the grass. 'He wanted to see it, so I showed him.'

'And he just happened to fall in, did he? Just like that?'

'Yes,' said Tig, at the same time as Herc said, 'No. He wasn't feeling very well.'

'Bad luck,' observed Arfur, his eyebrow still raised, as though it had got stuck halfway up his forehead.

'Heart attack,' said Tig.

'The poison probably didn't help,' reflected Herc. 'I think that was when he got really wobbly.'

Arfur's other eyebrow gave up waiting and climbed to join the first. 'Poison, eh?'

'Yes,' explained Herc patiently. 'We made poisonous tea. And I reckon he was still woozy from being hit on the head by the really heavy wooden— Ow! Tig, stop pinching me!'

She placed a hand over his mouth, which he knocked away crossly but fell silent. Tig spoke slowly, deliberately. 'It's important Arfur knows it was an accident, so he doesn't say any different to anyone else. I'm sure Arfur remembers that we have *lots* of money to help him understand that it was just a terrible, awful mistake.'

Arfur winked. 'Course it was. I know how you was all really looking forward to meeting him. It ain't your fault you accidentally whacked him over the head, accidentally poisoned him, and then accidentally drowned him in a pool of poo. Especially after Miss Happyday's accidental fatal injury and accidental burial six feet under the garden. Could have happened to anyone.' He winked again.

'Will you stop winking! It *was* all accidental,' Tig seethed.

'Except the burying under the garden bit,' corrected Herc. 'We did that on purpose. But my sister said it's OK if you do it to people who have very sadly passed away. You have to stand there after and give a speech to say exactly what you thought about them. We had a sing-song and everything, it was great.'

Tig began to feel desperate. 'OK, I know that sounds bad but—'

'Listen.' Arfur spread his hands wide. 'Far be it from me to judge. But as a friend, I'll tell you what I'll do. I'll help you with the bit of paperwork you'll need to get DEATH off your back. Let's go inside. Wouldn't mind a cuppa tea – it's a long climb up here.' He paused, and eyed the children sideways. 'Think I'll make it meself though, no offence.'

Tig looked askance at him, her suspicion raised by the idea of him doing anything as a friend. 'Paperwork?'

'Yep. That's all they'll want. Give us that briefcase there. It'll have all his forms in. We'll fill in the one that says he's done the inspection and it's all good, you take it down to Maisie – she can pop it in her cart, get it to DEATH HQ before they know what's what.'

'Uh . . .' Tig hesitated. Arfur seemed to know an awful lot about DEATH paperwork for a con man. She didn't quite believe it, partly because she didn't want to. She could imagine Stef's face if he learned they could have just ticked a few boxes on a piece of paper instead of . . .

'No need,' Herc chipped in. 'We've sorted it. Stef has gone to St Cod's to pretend to be Mr Fleetham!' He handed Arfur the inspector's schedule.

'Herc! Stop telling Arfur everything!' Tig hissed. 'We can't trust him, all right?'

But it was too late. Arfur's eyes were round as saucers at this news, as he scanned the paper.

'You sent that lad down to St Cod's? Are you out of your minds?'

'We gave him a *moustache*,' Herc announced reverently, as though this was the same as equipping him with body armour, a crossbow and a pair of pistols.

'I'll be blowed. You kids!' Arfur was lost in wonder. 'He's gonna get the surprise of his life, I reckon.'

'Why?' asked Tig, her stomach lurching. Surprises were not good, in this context.

A sly smile appeared on Arfur's face. 'You'll see soon

enough. Wish I was a fly on the wall of St Cod's right now.'

She glowered at him. 'You're bluffing. You don't know anything.'

'Me? I never lie. Not to me friends, anyways. Come on, now, let's get this form done. Easy as falling off a log, when you know how.' He lifted Mr Fleetham's briefcase from the ground and it bumped across the body, pulling Tig's coat off the inspector's head.

Arfur froze. As Tig watched, the smugness that was a permanent feature of his face disappeared. He gazed at the dead man for a moment, looking utterly confused, and then very worried.

'But *this* . . . Now this IS a problem. This ain't no inspector. This here is Tiberius Snepp. He works for Ainderby Myers. Or at least he did.'

Herc squealed. 'From the Mending House? Did he come to Mend us?'

Arfur was shaking his head slowly. 'There's only one thing Snepp normally does, but looks like you did it to him first. What the blazes was he up to here, dressed up as an inspector? It don't make sense. Unless . . . he was looking for something.' Sudden realization seemed to hit him like a slap in the face. 'Uh-oh. The Guvnor don't know she's dead. But what he does know is . . . Quick, gimme the rest of them papers.' He began to search frantically through them, skimming the pages. There was a floor plan of St Halibut's, and a short set of instructions, which he began to read, muttering. 'Oh no no no no. I never thought they'd be so stupid. How could they be so stupid?'

'Who? Who's been stupid? What have they done?'

He stuffed the papers in his pocket. His voice was shaky. 'You better come inside. I got things to tell you.'

Tig searched Arfur's face for some clue as to what he was up to, but at this moment he was unreadable. Was he telling the truth about Snepp? As someone who often worked for the Guvnor himself, he would know. And that was the problem: Arfur was not their friend, no matter what he said. There was some angle here that she didn't understand.

'Are we in trouble?' asked Herc. 'Is DEATH going to be cross with us?'

'You're in trouble all right,' said Arfur, as he pulled them into the house. 'But DEATH is the least of your worries.'

Ainderby Myers did not like to be kept waiting, whether for lunch, or for answers, or for money, or for justice.

Today, all of them were late.

The meal should have been here ages ago, and he was already pondering an appropriate punishment for the Mended whose job it was to bring him his pork sausages with apple sauce, roasted potatoes and onion gravy.

But that was nothing compared to the fact that he hadn't heard from Snepp. The wait was driving him mad. If Snepp returned empty-handed there would be nothing else for it but to overrun the place by force and make a real mess. It would be a lot of work to keep that quiet – people would ask questions.

Perhaps he should have known that the matrons of St Halibut's and St Cod's would try to get back at him eventually. He had been taking more and more of their orphans whenever he wanted, and he knew that it annoyed them. But he had never imagined that two such self-absorbed people as Miss Lackspittle and Miss Happyday would team up to do something about it. Somehow his worst nightmare had come true and they had found out who he really was, and worse . . . what he had done. He had not expected them to gather actual evidence, though. It disturbed him to think that he had somehow left a trail, when he had always been so careful.

The thought crossed his mind that perhaps Arfur had betrayed him. But he dismissed it. Both those harpies despised Arfur and would sooner kiss a frog than collude with him. Besides, Arfur had nearly as much to lose as Myers did if the past was unearthed. He would be horrified to think that they were both at risk of being exposed. If one thing was certain, it was that Arfur would always look out for himself at the expense of everyone else; he had proved that long ago. It was for this very reason that Myers had not told Arfur he was being blackmailed – the last thing he needed was for Arfur to panic and start trying to save his own skin.

But it didn't matter how the matrons had found the evidence; the problem was that just over two months ago they had threatened to reveal it to DEATH and the world, knowing it would end his career. In return for their silence, they had insisted that he leave their orphans alone, permanently. And they had demanded a quite outrageous sum of money. They had also been clever, holding one piece of evidence each. They'd threatened Myers that if he ever 'did something' to one of them, the other would run straight to DEATH and tell all. They had him sewn up good and proper, or so they thought.

Myers had pretended to graciously admit defeat and agree to their demands, and the money had been dispatched immediately. And then they'd gone quiet – very quiet – probably enjoying their newfound wealth. Presumably, they thought that would be the end of it.

They didn't know him at all.

He had begun his plans instantly, but it had taken time to lay them properly, and more time to acquire a DEATH inspector ID for Snepp. It had to be convincing, or the game would be up. It was essential to do it right first time – if he acted too hastily, they would be alerted, and his mistake would cost him everything. Once Snepp was inside St Halibut's and then St Cod's, he would find whatever evidence they had, and the blackmail money, with the matrons none the wiser. When it was all safely back in the Mending House, he would return and deal with the two of them.

Myers was very much looking forward to that part of the plan.

The door opened and a sackcloth-hooded figure with a tray tripped over the threshold. The plate shattered; sausages, gravy and apple sauce splattered over the cream rug. A drop of gravy landed on Myers' expensive leather shoe. The small girl's gaunt face held no terror, only exhaustion. Thin whistling rasps came from her throat as though she were breathing through a straw. With a pang of irritation, Myers recognized her: his burglar.

'You utterly useless waste of space,' he said in a low, emotionless tone. He had found that, usually, there was no need to shout. In fact, threats and fury were far more effective delivered quietly – it meant his victims were constantly anticipating further punishment. He was very good at that – plucking their nerves till they vibrated with fear the whole time. Like playing the harp. How he loved the music it made.

Ainderby sighed. The only problem with the Mended was that so many of them weren't much good for anything anymore. Pneumonia and a myriad of other diseases were interfering with the productivity of his workers.

He took a mint from the jar on his desk and popped it into his mouth. He noticed the Mended girl had drawn herself up to her knees, still wheezing, and was staring in that blank way they all had, out of the window. St Halibut's rose above the rooftops in the distance. He felt its very existence as an insult.

He was about to turn away when something caught the edge of his vision.

Someone was coming down the hill. Ah, finally, Snepp, on his way to St Cod's. *Late.* He recognized the hat.

Except, now he was paying attention, although it was Snepp's hat, the person under it definitely wasn't Snepp. Myers knew the sliding shuffle of his walk, as if he were creeping up on someone – which he often was. The person coming down from St Halibut's was slump-

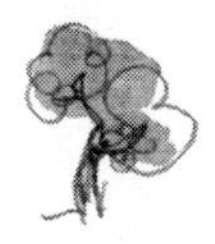

shouldered, hands in pockets and kicking at stones, a sulk in human form. A boy. He watched for several minutes as the figure reached the bottom of the hill and headed towards him. At first he thought the boy was coming straight to the Mending House. But then he turned aside at the last minute and knocked at the door of St Cod's.

Myers' cheek hollowed as he sucked the life out of the mint. This was unexpected. And very wrong.

He glanced back at the Mended girl, who, to his surprise, had stopped wheezing and managed to struggle upright again. She turned her eyes on him, dark and cold. Shocked, he felt the tiniest squirm of alarm. Ridiculous. But there was clearly more life remaining in her than he had thought.

Perhaps, before she conked out entirely, she might do something useful.

Chapter Sixteen

Stef's thoughts kept adding up to one, unavoidable answer.

There could be no doubt now that the St Cod's children weren't sick. They had been eaten.

Miss Lackspittle would never pass a real DEATH inspection, and she must know it. That would explain why she was making so little effort to impress him.

Which meant that she had no intention of letting him leave.

'What are you doing in here?' came the matron's harsh voice from the kitchen doorway.

'Nothing,' said Stef, whipping round. He felt a pop in his nose, and the telltale tickle of blood beginning a path down it, pooling into the cotton wads.

Miss Lackspittle's frame filled the entire doorway. Now he saw that her hands were distinctly red, as though he had interrupted her work in this kitchen when he

rang the doorbell. *Cannibal or zombie?* flashed through his mind.

'There's something not right about you, "Inspector".' He didn't like the way she put air quotes around that word. 'That ID you got. The picture under the skeleton logo. Doesn't look much like you.'

Stef regarded his chest. The card had worked its way out from under his shirt and was hanging there for all to see. She reached out and yanked it; the chain broke and she peered at it more closely. He swallowed, but his throat was dry. 'I've had a haircut.' As he spoke, he felt the stream of blood dislodge his Pamela-hair moustache. He put a hand up to grab it, too late. It fell to the floor between his feet, where it lay like a fatally wounded hairy caterpillar. He threw his arm across his face to hide his scar, which would surely jog her memory.

Miss Lackspittle was looking him up and down

with renewed interest. 'You know what? I don't think you're an inspector at all. I think you're a snitch. Dunno where from, but I'm sure I recognize you.'

Stef wanted to deny it but found his jaw muscles had locked in fear.

'And that leaves me with a problem. You see, if you *are* an inspector, you'll get me in trouble, and I can't let you leave. And if you're *not* an inspector, you're up to no good, and I can't let you leave. D'you see?' She kicked out behind her and the door clicked shut. 'So which is it?'

Stef considered both his options. Neither struck him as good as option number three: her letting him leave and forgetting any of this ever happened.

If he was a different sort of person, the sort most people expected him to be when they saw the size of him and his jagged scar, Stef would probably fight his way out of the door. But he'd never hit anyone in his life, he wouldn't know where to start – did the thumbs go inside or outside the fist? Were you supposed to punch straight, up, or down? He imagined his knuckles against the soft skin of Miss Lackspittle's nose, and knew he could not do it. There were the sort of people who could punch someone in the face, and then there were the sort of people who liked to eat cucumber sandwiches in neat triangles, with the crusts cut off, and he was one of those.

He let his arm drop, revealing his face. 'Please don't hurt me. I'm not an inspector. My name is Stef, and I live in St Halibut's. Miss Happyday died two months ago and we just—'

Miss Lackspittle's eyes were wide. 'I *knew* I recognized you! You're having me on.'

Stef managed a small head shake.

The matron looked shocked for a moment, and then began to laugh. She laughed for so long that Stef began to wonder if he might be able to escape past her while she was weak with giggles. Then finally she gathered herself. 'Well I never.'

She started to perform a strange wriggling dance, and then something happened that made no sense.

Miss Lackspittle's head and shoulders leaped from her body.

As the room began to swim before his eyes, he realized that he'd been more right than he knew: she was both a zombie *and* a cannibal.

And then he passed out.

Chapter Seventeen

Stef's vision blurred as he came round. He slowly became aware that he was lying on the floor in the kitchen at St Cod's. Two children were standing over him. One was a cross-looking boy of about eleven, who looked slightly familiar, and the other was a girl with the same face as Miss Lackspittle, but half her height. The two of them were startlingly thin, their legs like knobbly wigs. The girl was berating her companion furiously. 'What did you keep poking me for, Cuthbert? You

nearly gave us away soon as we opened the door!'

The boy huffed in outrage. Unlike the girl, when he spoke his accent was clipped and precise, with long vowels, as though he'd been brought up in a royal household.

'Me? I say, how dare you, Nellie Parker? You were wiggling around on my shoulders so much I thought you must have eels in your pants. Anyway, it wasn't me who forgot I was sucking a lolly in front of a DEATH inspector.'

'Well, he's not a real one, is he? And by the way, we practised that – you keep yer hands to yerself *inside* the coat, cos three arms ruins the disguise, remember? If this bozo weren't so stupid he would've noticed. You nearly knocked me teeth out when you whipped it out like that. And he fell for the Brussels sprout line, anyway. What a waste of a good lolly.'

'I'd like to remind you, *I'm* the one who jolly well found that lolly in the gutter.'

'We share everything, you know that. But forget it. When this St Halibut's scumbag wakes up, he's got some explaining to do.'

Stef had been too woozy to speak throughout this exchange, but now found the question that troubled him most. He sat up carefully, dried blood cracking uncomfortably on his top lip, and tried to focus around the room. 'Where did Miss Lackspittle go? Who are you two? Did she bite me? Am I undead?'

'Yes, you're undead,' said Cuthbert. 'Or, as most of us would put it, "not dead".'

Nellie squinted at Stef with distaste. 'Not the sharpest tool in the box, are you?'

Cuthbert appeared to feel sorry for him, and explained, 'Our matron lost the plot and ran off about two months ago. Whenever someone comes to the door, Nell gets on my shoulders and we give them a scare.'

Stef's brain was peddling furiously, but the meaning of their words was accelerating away into the distance. 'Your matron . . . did she eat some cake just before she disappeared, by any chance?'

Nellie looked impressed. 'Yeah! How d'you know that? Stuffed her face with a chocolate cake. I st— *borrowed* half of it off one of your lot, but she got to it first. Dunno what was in it, but she was buzzing like a swarm of drunk bees. It was like her brain went on holiday. Stuffed all her knick-knacks into a suitcase and said she was gonna join the travelling circus,' she added. 'Had some crackpot idea she was going to get a new job as one of the performing monkeys. We wouldn't have minded, but she took every penny in the house.'

Cuthbert sniggered. 'She didn't last long, from what we heard. Tried to swing without a safety net while juggling bananas and . . .'

Nellie whistled and dived her hand downwards. 'Banana split.'

Stef asked, 'Does anyone else know?'

'Arfur, cos he don't miss much, but no one else.'

'Arfur knows?' Stef was staggered. 'He didn't say anything to us.'

She smirked. 'Course not. I'd have his guts for garters if he did. He only found out a few days ago, anyway.'

According to Nellie, they had been all right without their matron at first. But Miss Lackspittle had taken everything of value with her. The children could only eat what was already in the larder, and whatever they could steal. Winter was approaching, the coal ran out, and there was no money for fuel. And so first the dining-room table had been chopped up and used to make a fire, and then the chairs. Then all the furniture including the beds, and the skirting boards, and anything else that would burn.

'Don't try going up the stairs,' Nellie warned. 'There aren't any. We had to start on the floorboards. It hasn't been easy for us.' She raised a scornful eyebrow at him. 'Not like you, by the look of it. Nice and well-fed, aren't you?'

'St Halibut's has a garden,' said Stef defensively. 'We grow vegetables. And we have a goat, for milk.' It felt like the wrong time to mention all the other luxuries they could afford with Miss Happyday's loot. Guilt sent his hand delving into a pocket. It came up with a slightly squashed piece of chocolate that he vaguely remembered Maisie giving him. The St Cod's children's eyes nearly popped out of their heads when he broke it in two and handed them half each.

Nellie spoke through a blissful mouthful. 'We only get what we can steal here in town, or what gets dropped in the dirt. Like that lolly.'

A penny dropped somewhere in Stef's brain. He pointed at Cuthbert. 'You were in the bakery. You stole my coin!'

'Nah, that was me,' broke in Nellie. 'I remember you now, tripped right over me. Cuth wouldn't have been able to get nothing off you. Been trying to teach him to be subtle and quiet like, but it's hopeless. Might as well give him a trumpet and a pair of cymbals. There's no sneak to him. That's the problem with coming from a rich family – they can't help but strut around like they own the place, even when they've not a penny to their name no more. His parents used to own half of Garbashire before they got banished.'

'A third, actually,' clarified Cuthbert modestly. 'But it was the best third.'

Now that Stef knew how desperate they had been for food, he *had* to ask . . . 'Where are the other children? St Cod's Home for Ingrates and Wastrels used to have more than this.'

Nellie shrugged. 'Not now. I'm the Ingrate and he's the Wastrel.'

Cuthbert frowned at her. 'I thought I was the Ingrate.'

'Mate, if anyone's a Wastrel it's you. You can't even steal a pastry. Besides, you ever seen me say "thank you" to anyone? I'm as ingrateful as they come. I'm the boss of Ingrates.'

Stef had to know if his hunch about the other orphans was true. Now that there were two little kids rather than one giant matron, he felt more confident about being able to get away in the event of attempted cannibalism. 'Did you . . . did you do something awful, when you were desperate?' He indicated their hands, red-stained.

Cuthbert held them up. 'This? Oh, yes. We made a bit of a mess, didn't we? Thank goodness it was only you, and not a real inspector. It's horrible, isn't it? I mean, who wants to eat that? But we had no choice.'

Stef felt sick. He was pretty sure, if it came down to

it, that he couldn't bring himself to eat another person. Not even a nibble.

'They're hard to chop,' Cuthbert pointed out. 'You try to hold them down and they're rolling all over the counter.'

'I can imagine.' Stef's breakfast was threatening to come out the same way it had gone in that morning. He had thought for a moment he'd found some friends to help with their inspector situation. But he had to get out of here right now. These were not children. They were monsters.

'We can't stand beetroot. But it's the only vegetable we've been able to get hold of for three weeks.'

Stef hardly dared breathe. 'That's . . . *beetroot* juice? Oh! Thank goodness!'

Nellie wrinkled her nose. 'What did you think it was?'

'Nothing,' he said quickly. 'Tomatoes, maybe.'

'So. You'd better tell me exactly what you were doing down here pretending to be a DEATH inspector. Because I don't mind telling you, I was that close to cleaning your clock. Still might, actually.'

Stef threw Cuthbert a blank look. 'Um. That sounds generous of you. Weird, but generous. Actually I, er, don't have a clock with me.'

'She means she was going to hit you,' Cuthbert

supplied. 'It's street talk. You'll get used to it.'

There was a noise at the door, making them all start.

Nellie checked through the kitchen window, and grabbed Cuthbert's hand. They moved across the room with such speed that before Stef could scramble up from the floor, they were gone.

'Hey! Where are you going?'

He followed them, struggling to keep up.

As he crossed the darkness of the hall, a shaft of light moved swiftly across the floor in front of him; the front door was opening. Whoever it was, Nellie and Cuthbert didn't want to meet them, and that was good enough for him.

Stef leaped across to the door, sprinted through the bare living room he had inspected earlier and wrenched open the opposite door.

They hadn't been kidding about the stairs.

He cast a panicked eye over the balustrade hanging vertically from the wall, the meagre pile of broken planks underneath it, calculated the distance from where he stood to the upper floor, and dismissed the idea of trying to reach it. He had never mastered forward rolls, let alone the sort of gymnastics that would be required here.

The sound of steps behind him.

Slowly he turned, knees weak.

'You must come to the Mending House.'

Stef peered fearfully into the shadow under the sackcloth hood. He could just make out the face of a girl. One of the Mended.

'There . . . there must be some mistake. We're not down for Mending.'

'We?' The girl's voice rattled with phlegm. 'Who is we? Your friends left by the back door. Besides, I didn't come for them.' She reached out with a bony hand. 'It's you I'm here to collect.'

Stef thought about trying to barge past her, but she had a firm grip now on his shirt collar. He tried to twist quickly away, but only managed to half choke himself. The girl might be thin, but she was all muscle.

The urge to fight dribbled out of him. She was right; there was no sign of Nellie and Cuthbert. They had left him to his fate. And so had Tig.

Chapter Eighteen

Arfur sat at the kitchen table in St Halibut's with Tig and Herc, and told them about the Guvnor.

Ainderby Myers was not his original name, for a start. As a child, he had been Burton Coggles, a poor boy who lived in rural Rankshire until one unlucky day his hunger got the better of him, and he was caught stealing apples from the neighbouring farm.

The local Mending House was a corn mill, turning grain into flour, and Coggles was put to work there. The one-legged governor, the *real* Ainderby Myers, was not a cruel man. He simply did what DEATH told him to do, which was work the children hard, and fill their heads with pointless knowledge. But the experience of being at the Mending House changed Coggles. Over the years, he grew bitter at the interruption of his life for such a small crime. Every day he obsessed over the injustice. He cultivated and nurtured his rage as though it

was a delicate plant in need of constant care. He became known for violent outbursts of temper, and the other children avoided him. This also meant that he was never considered Mended enough to leave.

On Coggles' eighteenth birthday, when he was due finally to be let out, there was an accident. Ainderby Myers fell into the hopper that Coggles was operating. Nobody saw exactly what happened, and when it was found that Coggles was missing too, it was assumed the same fate had befallen him. No one wanted to delve too thoroughly into exactly what had been smashed to bits by the machine's grinding stone.

'Just a sec, sorry . . .' Tig broke in. 'And you know this *how*, exactly?'

Arfur waved his hand at her dismissively. 'Used to live there, didn't I? Among other places. I get around. You wanna hear the rest or not?'

Tig found this very unconvincing, but nodded, and Arfur continued.

A few weeks later, hundreds of miles away on the other side of the country, a vacancy was posted for the job of Sad Sack Mending House Governor. Oddly, all the candidates but one dropped out; two actually dropped off a cliff. Identity checks of the winning applicant were made, of course. An official in Rankshire confirmed that, yes indeed, Ainderby Myers *had* previously been a Mending House governor there, and yes, he was considered to have done the job perfectly satisfactorily. Questions were asked, but since none of those questions was 'Is he dead?', and the officials didn't think to mention that quite important fact, everything was determined to be in order.

Now the new and improved Ainderby Myers set about wreaking his revenge on the world that had so abused him. His ruthlessness saw him grow in power, and in hatred. He vowed never to be poor again, and began accumulating wealth by any means. But his miserable empire was also his prison: so paranoid was he that someone might recognize him from the old days, so concerned that his deception would be exposed, that he could never leave the Mending House.

'Why are you telling us this now, if you've always known?'

'No reason to before. Why rock the boat? But reading Snepp's papers, it seems *somehow* your Miss Happyday and Miss Lackspittle found out, and instead of doin' the sensible thing and going straight to the authorities to dob him in, they went and did the stupidest, most brainless, literally the thickest—'

'WHAT?'

Arfur took a deep breath. 'It looks like they told him what they'd found, and went and blackmailed him instead.' He drew out of his pocket the crumpled paper that had come from the briefcase. Snepp's instructions were to visit both orphanages, retrieve all the money, and hunt for papers that contained any mention of Ainderby Myers. Once these were found, he would return and bring in the matrons for punishment. 'I thought the Guvnor was a bit twitchy when I saw him earlier. This explains it. He's expecting his man to come back down that hill any minute. He's probably watching.'

Tig grew cold.

'And now you've sent your pal down all dressed up, you've gone and let the worms out the bag. Or opened a tin of cats. Or whatever. Get this: until Myers finds what he wants and gets it back, he won't stop. And whatever it is, it's still here somewhere.'

Tig had expected a long search, but it hadn't taken more than a few minutes to find what they were looking for among Miss Happyday's papers – Arfur had seemed to know exactly what it would be. It was an article from the *Rankshire Gazette* ten years ago detailing the fatal 'accident' at the local Mending House, accompanied by a full-length sepia photograph of a man who most definitely was not the current Ainderby Myers, unless his right leg had grown back.

'So, that's where it came from – all that money we found when Miss Happyday died,' Tig said. 'I mean, we knew she wasn't poor, but when we found it after the accident, it did seem like an awful lot.'

Arfur whistled softly. 'Your Miss Happyday was lucky she died the way she did, nice and quick. Not like what the Guvnor would've done to her if he'd got his hands on her. Only reason you lot are still alive is he don't know she's dead. Yet. Same as he don't know Miss Lackspittle's out of the picture an' all.'

Tig gasped. 'You're kidding. The matron of St Cod's is dead too? Don't tell me library shelves fell on *her* as well?'

Arfur shook his head. 'Circus accident. She ran off about the same time your matron got squashed, must have realized blackmailing the Guvnor was too dangerous. Turned out so was the circus.'

Tig put her hands on her hips. 'And just when were you going to tell us that?'

Arfur shrugged, preoccupied, and she pursed her lips. She was still far from sure he could be trusted, and was very uncomfortable that he'd now seen where the money was. It hadn't escaped her notice how his eyes had lit up at the treasure hoard while they'd been searching for Miss Happyday's evidence. But there seemed little choice. And she needed to know more from him, without frightening her brother. She whispered in Herc's ear, 'This article is too important to leave lying around. Put it back under Miss Happyday's bed right now, with the money, and lock the door so we know it's safe.'

For once Herc didn't ask questions – something about Tig's tone had taken all the wind out of his sails. He scuttled from the room, holding the newspaper article out in front of him as if it were the crown jewels.

'Whatever evidence Lackspittle had, she took it wiv 'er. So what you got is all that's left.'

'How do you know?' Tig asked him, with narrowed eyes.

'When they told me Miss Lackspittle'd gone, I 'ad a little poke around around St Cod's. Just to see what was what, you know?'

'I bet you did. Arfur . . . I'll probably regret this, but I'm going to believe you. So, what will the Guvnor do next, when he realizes Snepp isn't coming back?'

The con man couldn't meet her gaze. 'Knowing him . . . you need to leave. And quick. Better give me that *Gazette* article . . .'

No doubt he was thinking Ainderby Myers would reward him well for retrieving it. 'We'll wait till Stef gets back and then—'

'Stef's not coming back,' came a voice from the doorway. Tig whirled round to see two children in St Cod's uniforms. 'He's been taken for Mending.'

All the blood drained from Tig's face.

Arfur gaped. 'Nellie? Cuth? What happened?'

The girl nodded at him. 'All right, Arfur?'

She filled them in quickly on the events at St Cod's, dumping the DEATH ID card with its broken chain on to the kitchen table. Arfur was telling Nellie about the blackmail when Tig got to her feet, trembling, indignant. 'And you just let Stef be taken? How could you? That's typical St Cod's, that is . . .'

''Ere.' Nellie stamped her foot. 'No point in us all

getting caught, is there? We came up to tell you, so don't be grumpy.' She glanced around. 'Ooh, this is quite nice, innit, Cuth? Let's stay here instead.'

There was a squeal from Herc, who had reappeared after his errand, slightly out of puff. 'Yes! Stay! I'd better make a cake if we're having so many visitors. Take a seat.'

Tig bit back her retort that they'd need no encouragement to take anything, what with their tendency to steal whatever wasn't nailed down.

'Listen, kids, no one should be staying,' Arfur said. 'You don't know Myers like I do. He won't just let this go once he finds out, and he might already have. When he handed your matrons that money he had no intention of letting 'em keep it. He's laid his plans, and when he knows they've failed, it's not gonna be pretty.'

'We're not going anywhere without Stef,' Tig snapped at him. 'I don't suppose you've ever had a friend, so you wouldn't understand.'

Arfur looked stung, but shut his mouth.

To Tig's amazement, Nellie agreed with her. 'Yeah. He was all right, your mate. Gave us chocolate, of his own free will. Seems a shame to leave him in there with that creep Myers. We could do what the matrons did,' she suggested. 'You know, blackmail him.'

Arfur snorted. 'What, because it worked out so well for *them*?'

Tig didn't even look at him. 'Don't recall asking for your opinion.'

'How about a swap?' suggested Cuthbert. 'He gives you Stef, and we give him that newspaper article if he wants it so much.'

Tig considered this. 'He'll want the money as well.' Although without it, they'd struggle to survive. 'It's worth a try.'

Arfur was adamant. 'Don't—'

She stopped him with a glare, and marched up the stairs to Miss Happyday's room, trailed by Herc, Nellie and Cuthbert.

'Tig,' Herc was saying, 'You'll never guess what—'

'Not now, Herc. Let's count the money, see what we've—' Her voice stopped mid-sentence. She was looking at the underside of Miss Happyday's bed. 'It's gone!'

All that was left were a few stacks of coins – small change. The bags of notes, and the article, were nowhere to be seen. Herc was prattling on and patting her elbow. She shook him off. She tried to think when Arfur had left the room, but felt sure he hadn't. Then out of the corner of her eye: Nellie and Cuthbert.

'Right, you two. Hand it over. Now. You pickpockets just can't help yourselves, can you?'

'I *beg* your pardon?' said Cuthbert, stiffening.

Herc was tugging at her sleeve. 'Did you not hear a single thing I said, Tig? I've sorted it.'

She turned to her brother warily. 'What?'

'You said Arfur couldn't be trusted, so I was clever and decided to move it to a safe place while you were talking with him. That newspaper article, and the money.'

Relief flooded through her. He could hardly have taken it far; he'd been out of the room less than fifteen minutes. She tutted impatiently. 'Well, where is it?'

He grinned. 'Somewhere no one would ever find it if they didn't know.'

'We don't have time for games, Herc. Just tell me.'

'Fine,' he huffed. 'It's hidden in the straw in Pamela's shed.'

His words settled for a moment before their meaning slowly seeped through to her.

'Oh, Herc, no.'

Chapter Nineteen

Several things hit Stef the moment he stepped into the cavernous factory room in the Mending House.

First was the noise. He wasn't sure what he'd expected – quiet rows of children bent over desks, perhaps, twisting raw cotton into yarn.

His ears filled with screeching and clanging as huge machines heaved back and forth, rows of them across the entire floor. In between, dozens of Mended children scurried about, fingers dipping in and out as steel whipped towards them, heads bobbing under, arms cranking levers, legs staggering under the weight of large numbers of full bobbins.

Everything was blurred. At first he thought it was snowing, and blinked up at the vaulted ceiling high above, wondering how such a thing was possible. But the room was hot, and heavy with moisture. Whenever he

moved, fluff twisted away – cotton, everywhere. The air was thick with it. His throat tickled with fibres, his nose tingled with the beginning of a sneeze.

'You have one more chance,' Ainderby Myers said, very close at his side. Stef felt his breath on his ear. 'Or this is where you will stay.'

Stef glanced around. Nobody was paying him any attention; none of the children seemed in the least bit curious about the new arrival. He scanned their faces for any familiar ones, perhaps Mary, or Eric, who'd been taken from St Halibut's only a few months ago. But there was no sign of them.

'You will tell me what has happened at St Halibut's, and what you were doing at St Cod's just now.'

Stef felt weak, his stomach lurching. He tried to say, 'Nothing,' but it came out as a whisper that was instantly sucked into the maelstrom around him.

Myers nodded, as though in sympathy. 'Perhaps I haven't made myself clear. If you do not tell me, I will have all of your friends . . . taken care of. Where is my man, who came to you this morning?' He pinched the brim of Snepp's hat from Stef's head, and turned it carefully in his hands. 'I will not ask you again.'

'*Your* man?'

Myers sighed impatiently at his blank look. 'The man who claimed to be an inspector. Where is he?'

The truth hit Stef right between the eyes. 'He wasn't from DEATH at all. *You* sent him!'

'Yes, thank you,' Myers said acidly, 'for explaining that. Do you have any helpful contributions on other subjects? Perhaps you could tell me my own name, or what day of the week it is? Seeing as you are quite the expert on painfully obvious facts.'

The Guvnor's eyes were glittering with anger. What was needed was a very good lie, but Stef had no idea what the right lie would be, and he was probably the last person who could tell it convincingly, anyway. He could only stare at Myers with his mouth open.

'Very well. I shall find out for myself. I hope you were not fond of anyone up there.' He turned to a guard who was standing, more bored than ever, to one side. 'Set him to work, Jerkson . . . Donk . . . Buttly?' He appeared to settle on the right name and the guard lifted his chin. 'Don't let him slack.' Buttly yawned and shrugged.

'Wait!' Stef cried, desperately. 'Miss Happyday is dead. Everyone except me left when she died. I went down to St Cod's just now because I was lonely, but there was nobody there, either.'

Myers turned back to him with interest. He had already been informed that St Cod's was entirely empty, by the Mended child who had collected this boy. 'Really. And Snepp?' He sighed impatiently at Stef's blank look. 'The inspector?'

Stef swallowed. 'He . . . he also died. I just borrowed his hat because . . . because I was cold. He was killed by . . .' He racked his brains. 'By a wild goat. Which is also what killed the matron. And it's still there, so I wouldn't go near if I were you.'

The Guvnor was grinding his teeth. 'A wild goat?'

'Uh, yeah.' He could tell by the Guvnor's expression that this hadn't exactly struck fear into his heart. He dredged his brain for the most terrifying description he could think of. 'Like, a really, *really* cross one.' It didn't seem to do the trick. Stef supposed you had to have met Pamela to understand how pant-wettingly nightmarish a cross goat could be.

Myers had turned a dangerous shade of puce. A vein throbbed in his temple. Then an unpleasant smile appeared. 'I don't know what kind of trick you're trying to pull off, but Miss Happyday is mistaken if she thinks I am so foolish. Work a while. I'll be back later. I'm sure you will feel more inclined to talk soon.'

The work was hard, and the air so hot and heavy that Stef felt unnaturally tired – increasingly so, as though his very life was being sucked out through his pores. Although, looking around him at his fellow Mended children, Stef could see that he had been given one of the less dangerous jobs. He had to take off the full spindles, weighed down with their thread, and stack them, replacing them with empty ones. The scavengers had it much worse; these were generally the smaller children, the ones who could slip under the machines while they were working, gather up the stray fluff underneath, and nip out again as the mule came clanging back. There was to be no pausing of the machines. Buttly had told him that if ever they stopped during the day, there would be trouble.

It would be dangerous enough, he thought, if they were entirely focused, but they all looked half asleep. Most of the other Mended children had failed to respond to his whispered attempts to engage them in conversation when the guards' backs were turned, except for the odd nod or shake of the head. Nobody smiled.

He grabbed the arm of the girl next to him.

'Hey, what's your name?' he asked her.

She frowned and shrugged, as though he'd asked her to remember some trivial piece of history.

'Please be careful,' he begged her. 'You could get hurt.'

The girl barely paused in her work. 'Doesn't matter. Alive, dead – what's the difference?'

He was horrified. 'Of course there's a difference!'

Her gaze passed through him. 'Someone else would

replace me. The machines wouldn't stop. That's all that matters.'

Shocked into silence, Stef turned away and picked up another spindle with numb hands.

Misery began to creep upon him as the reality of his predicament became clear. They had all been fooled. He had failed in his mission, and now Myers was going to go and catch Tig and Herc too. It was all his fault, because he'd been slow, and stupid, and . . . He banged his fists on the empty bobbins in despair. One broke, and half of it rolled off behind a pile of sacking. He glanced round – luckily the guard was facing the other way – and quickly pocketed the broken shards before they were spotted.

‘I see what you’re doing,’ said a voice by his ear.

He sprang back. It was the kidnapping girl again.

‘Gathering materials for your escape. You won’t get anywhere that way. Hey, don’t worry,’ she reassured him, seeing his stricken face. ‘I won’t tell. Sorry about, you know . . . bringing you here.’

Stef was so glad to have someone to talk to who didn’t just look straight through him that he found it impossible to bear a grudge. ‘It’s OK.’ The guard was still looking away, and he grabbed the chance to ask what he’d been wondering since he arrived. ‘Where’s Mary, and Clarry, and Seema, and Eric? I haven’t seen them yet.’

She looked blank.

‘They used to be at St Halibut’s, but they got sent here. Eric came just a few months ago.’

He saw recognition come, then she looked away. ‘Oh. Yes. I remember him. He got sick. They all did. It happens a lot.’

He searched her face for an explanation.

‘I’m sorry. When they can’t work, Myers gets rid of them.’

Stef felt faint. ‘Gets . . . rid?’

‘He *says* they get taken to hospital.’ Her expression told him what she thought of that.

They were silent for a while, working side by side as a guard strolled by.

'Why aren't you . . . like them?' He nodded at the Mended, when they were alone in the row again.

She smiled for the first time and her eyes glittered. 'It's because the Guvnor's so greedy. I spend less time in the factory, since he gets me doing so many burglaries for him. I'm really good at it.' There was no pride in her voice, only bitterness. 'So I miss out on a lot of the hardest work, and the brainwashing the others get, but I make out like I'm no different. He says terrible things to them all the time, and it's hard not to take at least some of it in. You start to doubt yourself. I've tried talking to them, believe me, but it's only me, on my own, and they won't listen. They're scared of Myers; they think he's all-powerful. I'm Ashna, by the way. Are you sure you've forgiven me for kidnapping you?'

Stef decided to be generous. 'It's all right. I know you didn't have a choice.'

'Actually, I could have run off. I could have gone lots of times, whenever he sends me out. But I won't leave without them.' She gestured at the others. 'And the truth is, when he made me bring you in, I saw a chance, if I could get to you before you were properly Mended.'

'A chance?'

She put her mouth close to his ear so that it tickled. 'To get out of here. Every single last one of us.'

Chapter Twenty

Tig, not wanting to add goat bites to her worries, stayed outside Pamela's enclosure while Herc went in. But it was clear enough to see through the open shed door that their goat had enjoyed a feast. There were tiny scraps of torn pound notes across the grass outside, and more in the shed. Small, soggy and chewed fragments of paper money and, here and there, the remnants of a crucial ten-year-old newspaper article. Finally Herc emerged into the outside part of the enclosure, looking stricken. Pamela followed him out. 'I can't believe how much she's eaten. It's like she was starving.'

'Or just evil.'

Herc drew a protective arm around the goat, whose jaw was working lazily to one side as she observed Tig through narrowed eyes. The jagged corner of what looked like a ten-pound note dangled from her mouth. 'She's not evil. And she's really, really sorry, aren't you,

Pammy?' he insisted, stroking between her ears.

Tig exchanged a glance with the goat and confirmed her suspicion that it was not, in fact, possible to feel any less sorry than Pamela felt right now.

She threw up her hands. 'Well, that's it. Most of the money's gone, and the article – the only power we had over Ainderby Myers. We're doomed. Stef is doomed.'

'It's not *gone*,' pointed out Herc. 'I mean, it's just inside her. It'll come out again.'

'Herc.' Tig controlled her voice with some difficulty. 'Are you suggesting we wait for Pamela to go to the loo, and then tape it all together and present it to the Guvnor?'

Herc squinted at her. Sometimes it was hard to know when she actually wanted an answer. 'Maybe in a gift box?'

★

It was hard to find anything positive about their current situation; the chances of finding so much as a soggy one-pound note in Pamela's dung when it appeared were slim, let alone a perfectly preserved newspaper article. That didn't stop Herc from hoping. The others slumped at the table, heads in hands, while Herc stirred his cake mixture. Every now and then he fingered the ID card, which he had refastened round his neck, tying the broken ends together.

'The Guvnor could be here any minute,' Arfur warned them, though Tig noticed he made no move to leave himself.

'You know, Arfur, Myers will probably think *you* had something to do with the blackmail, seeing as you're the one that knows all about him,' she pointed out. 'Why don't *you* run away?'

'Never you mind about me,' he said, though judging by his chalky complexion, that very thought was playing on his mind. 'Myers'll have got everythin' out of Stef by now – he'll know your matron's dead, and he'll be gathering some thugs to come up. Probably once it gets properly dark, when no one will see them coming.'

Tig bit her nails and scowled. 'Shut up. I'm thinking.'

Herc grew philosophical.

'When you think about it,' he said, 'I reckon we've had a good, interesting life. Or if not *good*, then at least not bad. Although, parts of it *have* been quite bad – I mean, we've not had much money for most of it. And maybe not that interesting, either, seeing as we've never actually been anywhere outside Sad Sack. But at least we've had friends. Well, until most of them were snatched away and—'

'Stop, Herc. Just stop,' Tig pleaded.

'I just think we shouldn't be all hopeless and sad. I'm sure everything will work out. We're still young!'

'So, what you're saying,' said Cuthbert, 'is that our lives have been solitary, poor, nasty, brutish and short. Thanks. I feel so much better.' He dipped a finger in Herc's mixing bowl and sucked it sorrowfully. 'Nice. Could do with some raisins, though.'

Herc moved the bowl away. 'Please. Leave these things to the experts.'

'I just think—'

'Dried fruit shouldn't go anywhere near a chocolate cake. You're as bad as Tig. Last time she sneaked a load of raisins in, but I just picked them all out when she wasn't looking,' he added smugly.

Tig took a breath to snap that they had bigger problems than raisins, and then froze. 'That's it!'

Everyone regarded her warily.

'Sneak in, pick out!' No one responded, and she tapped the table impatiently. 'When Myers isn't looking! Get what I'm saying?'

'I think so . . .' Nellie said slowly. 'That you're a fruitcake?'

Tig didn't seem to have heard. She rose from the table, trembling with excitement. 'We break into the Mending House and get Stef out. The Guvnor won't be expecting that. Nellie can pick the locks on the side door – the one in the alley next to St Cod's. It leads into the kitchen – you can hear cutlery clanking behind the wall there.'

'Er . . .' said Nellie.

Tig talked over her. 'Once she's inside, Nellie will find Stef, and get him out the same way she came in.'

'What the blazes?' Nellie finally got a word in.

'How'm I supposed to get past all them guards?'

'That's *our* job,' Tig told her. 'We'll draw the guards out to the front, with some kind of distraction.'

'Who's *we*?' asked Cuthbert.

'You and me—'

'And me!' broke in Herc.

Tig opened her mouth to forbid him but immediately knew it was useless. At least if Herc was with her she could keep an eye on him. 'Fine,' she said. 'Me and Cuth and Herc—'

'And Pamela,' said Herc.

'No.'

'What's more distracting than Pammy?' he asked, and no one could disagree.

'Whatever. The important thing is that, meanwhile, Nellie and Stef slip out the side door, run round the back of the Mending House through the fields, and meet us at the crossroads. Then we'll all have to run for it. Not sure where. Maybe the woods, for a while.'

Herc gasped at the suggestion. 'Like Robin Hood! We could live there forever. A secret village! This is going to be *brilliant*!'

Tig's plan wasn't universally approved.

'Tell you what,' said Arfur. 'To save time, you could all just go down there and invite Myers to bump you off. End result'll be the same.'

'No one asked you, con man. He hasn't left the Mending House for years – he's scared to. That'll give us time.'

'Pfffft.' Arfur shook his head. 'Scared? He's not scared – he's just careful. He'll be here soon enough. And how come all your amazing plans involve sending someone else to do daft and dangerous things while you sit on your—'

'That is not true! I'm going to be distracting Myers – hardly safe, is it? Besides, it makes sense for Nellie to do it. If anyone can sneak in there, she can.' Tig couldn't quite meet Nellie's eye. She probably owed her an apology for earlier; perhaps flattery would do for now.

'Only one problem,' declared Nellie. 'I'm sneaky, I'll grant you that. But I'm a pickpocket, not a lock picker.'

'Bet you can't say that really fast,' said Herc.

Tig slumped a little. 'You don't know how to pick a lock?' This was an unforeseen flaw in her plan.

'How many pockets you know have locks on 'em? You want a burglar, not a pickpocket.'

As one, they turned to Arfur, who stopped the idea in its tracks. 'Count me out. When you all get caught it ain't gonna be my fault.'

Tig sniffed. She had expected no better from him.

'So that's it, then. None of us knows how to pick a lock.' Her heart sank. There were only so many plans she could come up with, and she was pretty sure she'd already scraped the bottom of the barrel.

'Apart from me, of course,' Cuthbert said modestly.

Nellie gaped at him, and then punched him none too gently on the arm. 'Get outta here. Where'd a posho like you learn to pick a lock?'

'My mother taught me, actually. You just need a stiff bit of wire. The right kind, used with skill, will open almost anything – even huge underground vaults with top security.'

'And your mum was . . . ?' asked Tig.

'Governor of the Bank of Garbashire, and Chief Officer of the Treasury.'

There was a short silence.

'I'm starting to see why they might have been a bit cross with your parents,' said Nellie.

'Never mind that,' Tig said excitedly. 'So, we'll just swap roles. Cuthbert will do the break-in, and—'

'He can't go on his own,' insisted Nellie. 'He'd mess it up.'

'How dare you,' said Cuthbert. 'You'd mess it up more.'

'You're not actually thinking about doing this?' Arfur

stood and banged his fists on the table, shouting, 'Don't you get it? Ainderby Myers don't mess about! He's already got your mate held hostage, and he's probably five minutes away from getting the rest of you. And you've got nothing against him now. Nothing. He's gonna Mend you all from your stupid heads to your stubborn little toes . . . or worse!'

There was silence in the kitchen. Tig imagined Stef, helpless, waiting to be rescued. She could not let him down.

Nellie had seemed reluctant up to this moment. She had never before risked life and limb on anyone else's behalf, not even Cuthbert's, and didn't intend to start now. However, neither had she ever refused a direct challenge to her pride.

She narrowed her eyes and crossed her arms over her chest. 'Yeah? Mend us, will he? I'd like to see him try.'

Chapter Twenty-One

Just as Ashna had predicted, at ten in the evening a bell rang, and all the Mended set about shutting down the spinning mules. The clanking subsided, leaving an echo that continued in Stef's ears, as though the work had merely moved inside his head for the night. Myers had retired to his quarters without drilling the children on their chants, seeming preoccupied.

The Mended silently formed lines and were filing, unasked, through the door that led into their dormitory.

Stef joined the end of the exhausted line, copying their slumped movements. It wasn't hard to fit in, to be honest – his back ached, and his eyelids drooped at the sight of the stone floor scattered with blankets. His mind, though, felt as though it was sparking with static, as it had been since he and Ashna had figured out the details of their plan in snatched whispers.

Every night, just as the factory was winding down, Ashna had told him, Myers would take a late supper of scrambled eggs and crusty bread, which Buttly brought to him on a tray in his study. From the same saucepan, the night guards would each get a small plateful. Tonight, those eggs would have a little extra ingredient.

Stef's eyes were wide. 'We're going to poison them all?'

'Not poison. Snorrington's Herbal Bedtime Snoozies from Powders 'n' Potions. Myers takes a pinch every night to help him sleep. He hasn't been paying attention to how much is left in the packet over the past few weeks.' She grinned. 'We're going to give them all a nice big dose. Enough to make sure they don't hear what we're up to.'

'And what are we up to?'

'Stealing the keys from Buttly. He has one set, chained to his belt. Myers has the only others. We'll let everyone out, and head for the woods. Once he finds everyone's gone, nowhere in Sad Sack will be safe.'

Stef was cheered by the idea of not having to spend a night in the Mending House, but of course he would go and get Tig and Herc first, before meeting Ashna and the others in the woods. They must be beside themselves with worry. Maybe they had guessed what had happened to him and were even planning a rescue. Though perhaps they had already fled. Part of him hoped so. The other part wanted to rescue *them* himself, and show them what he was capable of.

'How are you going to get the stuff into the scrambled eggs?' he'd asked.

'That's where you come in,' she'd told him.

Now that the time had come, the whole plan seemed too risky. But Ashna was already hiding in the kitchen, and if he didn't do what he was supposed to, she'd be in trouble.

Before Stef, last in line, reached the dorm, Buttly headed into the kitchen to make the scrambled eggs. There were no other guards left in the main room. They would be stationed around the courtyard, and probably outside the vault room upstairs that Ashna had mentioned.

It was now or never. Stef doubled back into the factory and ran, crouched over, to the nearest spinning mule. The nut he found unscrewed more easily than he was expecting and he winced at its tinkling as it hit the floor and spiralled away under the machine, but no one came to look. The next nut was harder, but he soon loosened it and stowed it in his pocket. Soon, every row of machines had several random nuts missing, levers in the wrong position.

Stef paused, holding his breath. Crouched next to the last row, he could just see Buttly moving around in the kitchen, whistling as he stirred the eggs.

Now for the tricky part. He was not used to moving very fast. But for this, he'd have to.

Hidden behind a barrel at one side of the kitchen, Ashna watched Buttly scratch at the back of his trousers with the wooden spoon and then go back to stirring the pot. He must be almost done by now. Stef had better hurry.

She felt the bag of herbs in her fist. Myers had stacks of them in his bathroom. He must have a lot of trouble sleeping. She couldn't sympathize; if he was tortured by nightmares, he deserved every one.

He only ever used a pinch. It must be pretty powerful stuff. But this was for several guards, plus Myers, and they would only get one chance. She decided to put the whole thing in.

But Buttly needed to leave the kitchen.

She felt a stirring of fear. Had Stef chickened out?

Now Buttly lifted the pan to his mouth, and his thick pink tongue came out, shovelling egg inside his maw.

'Ow!' he yelped as his tongue touched the hot metal of the saucepan. He dropped the pan back on the range and held his tongue between thumb and forefinger, searching around for something, anything, to ease the pain of the burn. Finally, his eye alighted on the door to the ice cellar, which had been freshly restocked with a delivery today, and he hastily rummaged inside and used both hands to pull out a huge cube of ice, which he pressed against his burning tongue.

Bliss slackened his features: but at last there came the sound of machinery from the factory floor next door. Buttly looked up, confused. It was the wrong time to turn it on, and it did not sound like it usually did. There was a horrible whining, grinding sound of gears crunching together.

Frowning, Buttly tried to put the ice cube down, but it appeared to be stuck to his tongue. After some frantic pulling, he left it dangling from his mouth and rushed from the room.

Ashna squeezed out from the behind the barrel and leaped for the pan.

★

Peeping round the dormitory door frame, Stef could see Buttly standing agog among the whirling machines, which were shedding loosened nuts and bolts as they jolted on misaligned wheels. The thug's look of absolute helplessness was compounded by the fact that for some reason his tongue was being dragged downwards out of his mouth by the weight of a large ice cube, which swung from side to side as his head turned to take in the scene, like an elephant's trunk.

Every row of machines was going like the clappers, the mules spinning and yanking threads at such a rate that they were breaking all over the place. A stray bolt pinged across and lodged in Buttly's left nostril like a metal bogey. Entire sections of machinery began to vibrate crazily and then spin. The noise was increasing in pitch and volume, and then, next to Buttly, a bobbin shot upwards like a rocket, spewing its load of thread like a spiderweb, which then drifted gently down over his shoulders. He pawed frantically at himself as if being attacked by a swarm of wasps. One by one, more bobbins popped off like champagne corks, flinging up great spools of thread. Buttly ran towards one machine, then another, in a panic, tripping over his own feet as the thread tangled between them.

Stef watched a shadow pass along the wall – Ashna. She slipped into the dormitory beside him and peeked out to watch. Behind them, the Mended were fast asleep.

'All done. Wow,' she said. 'That's certainly a distraction.'

They watched for an entertaining few moments until the door to the corridor was flung open and there stood Ainderby Myers. His mouth twitched as he took in the scene. Then he began moving quickly and efficiently among the machines, flicking levers, turning them off. When he had finished and the room was eerily silent, his shoulders were strewn with thread streamers.

'Get up,' he told Buttly quietly.

Buttly tried to clamber to his feet, slipped on the puddle of water that had been the ice cube, now freed from his tongue, and grabbed on to Myers for support. Myers shook him off viciously.

Buttly looked close to tears. 'The mathines wen crathy! Jutht thtarted up all by themthelves!'

Myers eyes closed, as though perhaps if he couldn't see his henchman, he might actually disappear. Then his nostrils flared. 'What is that smell?'

There was indeed an odd smoky aroma coming from the kitchen. Buttly's eyes widened. 'The thcrambled eggth!' He slipped on the puddle again in his haste to get to the kitchen and came back looking shamefaced. 'They're thlightly burnth. I tathted it and itth not too bad though.'

Ashna's breath caught. If Myers decided to make Buttly cook a new batch, their plan would be thwarted.

Myers sighed. 'You are a blithering nitwit. Clear this up. Any damaged thread will come off your wages.'

'But, whath abouth the thcrambled—'

'Have one of the Mended bring it to me.' He paused. 'The burglar can do it. I wish to speak to her.'

Despite his fatigue, there was no danger of Stef dropping off, especially after a yawning Buttly came to fetch Ashna from her blanket, where she too was faking sleep.

'Get up, burglar. You're wanted. Guvnor's got a job for you.'

Stef spent over half an hour staring at her empty space, expecting her to return after delivering the Guvnor's scrambled eggs, before he heard the distant clang of the Mending House gate and realized what that meant. Myers had sent her out on a burglary somewhere, with appalling timing.

He was on his own.

He took in the sleeping forms of the Mended around

him. They tossed and turned, coughing, wheezing. The girl on the next blanket made a whistling sound with every breath. His heart contracted painfully – she couldn't be more than six.

What would Tig do? He tried to think like her. He supposed . . . she would just do it. On her own. She wouldn't be sat here waiting for someone else to give her instructions.

Stef silently opened the dormitory door. There was moonlight coming through the high, small windows at the top of the factory room, lighting his way. He felt a surge of joy at seeing Buttly, slumped against a mule, snoring loudly. He must have fallen asleep mid clear-up. Stef prodded him with his shoe, gently, and then not so gently. Buttly drooped slowly sideways until his cheek was smooshed into the floor.

There was a large ring of keys attached to a chain on Buttly's belt, just as Ashna had said. After some failed attempts to remove them, Stef ended up unbuckling the belt and taking the whole thing.

Padding softly back to the dorm, he began to try to wake the other children. It was almost impossible. One would blink, bleary-eyed, and sit up, but by the time he'd moved to the next, the first had sunk down again into sleep.

'Get up!' he hissed as loudly as he dared. 'We're getting out of here!'

He even tried shaking them, but they were like rag dolls in his hands. It was infuriating. If Buttly was knocked out, the other guards probably were as well, and Myers too, assuming he had eaten the scrambled eggs. The plan had gone perfectly, except now he couldn't get anyone to leave. He had not anticipated this. For a moment he considered whether he might carry them out one by one, but dismissed the idea. He could not get forty Mended into the woods without help.

He could, though, just leave on his own.

The keys were cool in his hand, Buttly's belt dangling against his legs.

He could make it. If he was lucky, and fast, he could get up to St Halibut's and down again into the woods with Tig and Herc before anyone noticed he had gone.

In the kitchen, he tried the keys at random in the top lock of the door that led outside, into the alley next to St Cod's. The fourth one slid smoothly in. He turned it and felt it click. The bottom lock did the same.

He bit his lip and paused with his fist around the key in the final, middle lock. Someone in the dormitory was coughing till they gasped for breath.

Clamping his jaw against the tremendous wave of guilt, he turned the key.

One of the younger boys was crying softly in his sleep. They only ever cried in their dreams, Ashna had told him.

The handle was slippery with his sweat. He only had to push it down and he'd be free.

His forehead pressed against the door for a moment. And then he turned and walked deliberately back to the dormitory.

Chapter Twenty-Two

If anyone had glanced down the dark alleyway in between St Cod's and the Mending House, they would likely have seen nothing, since the moonlight did not penetrate far on this side of the building. If they peered very closely, they might, at most, have seen a very tall shadow, wobbling about by the Mending House side door.

'This is just like old times!' whispered Cuthbert cheerfully. 'Almost makes me nostalgic for the days of pretending to be Miss Lackspittle.'

'Way back in the old days of this afternoon, you mean?' retorted Nellie, her voice coming muffled from somewhere below. 'And I liked it better when it was *my* knee mashed up against *your* face, not the other way round.' She jerked her shoulder to move his weight. 'Why'd you have to start at the top lock, anyway? Shoulda done the bottom ones first. Get a move on, can't you?'

'Oh, do stop moaning, Nellie; you can be an awful bore sometimes.' He adjusted his position on top of her shoulders, and reinserted the wire carefully into the first lock on the imposing heavy wooden door. 'I really don't understand why it isn't working,' he huffed. 'It should sort of click, and then you know the lock's opened. Oh! I heard something then. I think that might have been it.'

'Gerroff! That was your heel on me teeth, you berk.' She spat out a piece of grit. 'All you're gonna break is me legs. Oi, stop jiggling around, you'll—'

Nellie staggered forward, catching Cuthbert's right shoe on the door handle, which pinged down. The door gave to their weight and creaked open, sending them both tumbling into the kitchen of the Mending House, sprawled across the floor.

Cuthbert sat up, rubbing his temples. 'So much for top security – it was just sitting there unlocked! It's a disgrace. Tax payers' money was spent on this rubbish.'

Nellie scowled. 'Shh! There'll be guards,' she hissed.

'Yes, there's one underneath me,' Cuthbert pointed out.

They both looked at the uniformed man, slumped face down, who remained unresponsive, even when Nellie held his head off the floor by his hair.

'Cor, look at that! We must've knocked him out cold with the door!' she whispered, wonderingly.

'Told you,' said Cuthbert. 'I'm *ever so* good at this.'

Chapter Twenty-Three

Ainderby Myers paced the floor through his quarters – bedroom and study – stopping every now and then to look through the window. He had put out both the candle on his desk, and the lamp on the mantelpiece, to better see into the darkness. The boy's ridiculous story had sent him into an agony of indecision and confusion. The tale had surely been cooked up by Miss Happyday. But to what purpose? Had she laid a trap for him up there? If he went to investigate, would he fall victim to something he had not anticipated? Or could there really be some truth in what her orphan had said?

And what of Miss Lackspittle? A loose thread if ever there was one. And yet . . . wherever Miss Lackspittle was, she clearly hadn't done anything to incriminate him, otherwise DEATH would have come knocking at his door by now. She must simply have lost her nerve and decided to flee.

But the continued absence of Snepp troubled him deeply.

Then a solution had come to him: to send his burglar, Ashna, up the hill to St Halibut's. She would be there by now, finding the evidence and the money, and the truth, for him. If no one was there, as the boy had claimed, all well and good. If Miss Happyday or any of her orphans were still about . . . well, his burglar was stealthy. He reflected that perhaps he should have sent Ashna in the first place, to remove it from under their noses silently – it was an operation perhaps better performed with a delicate instrument like her, rather than a sledgehammer like Snepp. But he had been angry, and wanted to hurt them, and it had clouded his judgement.

Being in the dark about what was going on up there was intolerable, like a horrendous itch he couldn't scratch. Briefly he considered leaving the Mending House for the first time in ten years, and going there himself, just to *know*. It was night-time, and hardly anyone was about. Anyone who did see him leave the gates of the Mending House would be too terrified to approach him, anyway – he had worked hard on his reputation in Sad Sack. And it was highly unlikely anyone would recognize him from the old days. Most people here had never even heard of Rankshire, let alone been there.

And yet . . . his own fear would not listen to reason. He felt its monstrous presence in a dark corner of his mind that he kept shut off. He could sense it thrashing about, hurling itself against its restraints. If he lost the Mending House, he would return to nothing. He would be poor again, except this time there would be no way back. He had terrible dreams, where he stepped outside and everything fell away from him into a void, and he himself tumbled down, into endless darkness and despair.

His stomach growled, and he shook himself. No, probably just indigestion.

Talking of which . . . He sighed as he looked at the congealed plate of scrambled eggs that the burglar had brought him over an hour ago. Stone cold, it smelt funny – presumably a result of being burnt – and resembled a plateful of vomit.

Nevertheless, he was hungry. He was too uptight to sleep. And there was nothing to be done until the girl returned from St Halibut's with his prize. The whole saga had gone on too long and now he was losing the threads of it. He sat down and gloomily chased a lump of egg on to his fork.

He was just raising it to his mouth when there was a commotion at the front gate – the bell clanged, the gate rattled as somebody pounded upon it. He snatched back the curtains at his study window and peered out.

There was a hysterical girl shaking the bars of the gate with both hands, a small boy holding some kind of placard, and . . . a white goat. He hurried to the door that led from his quarters into the corridor, and leaned out. 'Buttly! Handle that!'

Returning to the window, he blinked to clear his vision; the girl was still there, but he could no longer see the boy or the goat. Why on earth would there be a goat outside the Mending House, anyway?

He must be more tired than he'd realized.

He waited, but minutes later the girl was still causing a ruckus and no one came.

'Buttly!' he shouted. 'Donk! Jerkson! What do I pay you for, you lazy fools?'

Finally, he threw the fork and the plate to the floor, scattering egg across the carpet, relit the lamp and stalked out to deal with the disturbance.

Chapter Twenty-Four

'Free the Mended! Free the Mended!'

Tig was yelling at the top of her voice, windows were opening up on the opposite side of the street in the flats above the shops, and heads were poking out to see what the fuss was about.

Herc was marching back and forth in front of the gates with his placard, upon which he had written in large letters 'DOUWN WITH MENNDIG!' Pamela was following his progress with a beady eye, making occasional lunges at those watching above, teeth bared.

''Ere, pipe down, can't you?' shouted a woman from the window above the hardware store over the road.

'We're protesting against Mending,' Tig shouted back to her. 'It's wrong!'

The woman waved dismissively. 'Oh, come now, it can't be that bad. I dare say they deserve it. As will you if you don't let me get some sleep.'

TAXIDERMIS

Herc put his hands on his hips. 'I bet you don't really think that. You know bad things happen in there.'

The woman didn't deny it, but shrugged. 'Well, that's just how it is, so you'll have to lump it.'

'We will *not* lump it,' yelled Herc, indignant. 'We're sick of lumping it, and so should you be! If you all stopped lumping it and said something, he wouldn't be able to get away with it, and . . . and . . . there wouldn't be so many lumps!'

'What a lot of fuss,' came another voice from two windows down, above Powders 'n' Potions. Bickley Brimstone, in a striped nightcap, stuck his head out. 'You kids are far too noisy. At least those Mended ones are quiet!' He considered. 'Apart from the coughing. And the despairing sobbing at night. But aside from that, they're beautifully behaved. I'm all for it.'

'It's cruelty!' Tig yelled, and rattled the gate bars again. She desperately hoped Myers would be coming soon – Nellie and Cuthbert were probably trying to haul Stef out at this very moment. She could see one guard, but he appeared to be asleep, crumpled in a corner of the courtyard next to the inner door – quite a feat considering the noise they were making.

Finally, a door in the right wing of the building opened and Ainderby Myers strode towards the gate.

Tig had never seen him close up before – few people had, other than a glimpse over Maisie's shoulder as she handed him the mail – but there was no one else it could be. He wore a well-cut grey suit, his trousers flapping in the biting wind as he came towards her. She was reminded of how young he was – his face was unlined, but set hard.

She suddenly became aware of an absence beside her, and looked round. There was no sign of Herc, or Pamela. The placard lay abandoned in the street. Herc must have been frightened when Myers came out, and gone to hide somewhere nearby. At least, she hoped so. She redoubled her volume.

'Free the Men-ded, free the Men-ded!'

She had at least achieved one thing: the Guvnor looked astonished. 'What on *earth* do you think you're doing?'

'Protesting against Mending,' said Tig, with only a slight wobble in her voice. 'Society must speak out against this abuse.'

Myers' lip curled. 'Society?' He indicated the flats opposite with a jerk of his chin. The windows had all slammed shut as soon as he had appeared. 'Society wishes you would go home, little girl. Where do you live?'

'Never you mind,' she said, far more boldly than she

felt, glad that she had remembered not to wear the St Halibut's uniform.

His eyes flashed with anger and he took a step up to the gate, but then abruptly stopped. He appeared uncomfortable out in the open, even behind the Mending House railings. 'You're lucky I'm too busy to Mend you,' he told her, and turned to go back the way he had come. 'Keep this up and I might change my mind. Go home.'

'I won't!' she yelled after him, frantically shaking the gate again. She couldn't let him go back in yet.

'Guards!' snapped Myers, and only then seemed to notice the slumped shape on the ground. He frowned, then glanced sharply at Tig. His eyes bore into hers. 'Something is going on,' he murmured.

Without another word, he broke into a run, leaped over the guard, and disappeared into the main part of the Mending House.

Tig stared after him, stunned, unsure what to do next.

There was still no sign of Herc, or Pamela. She sprinted to the alley in between the Mending House and St Cod's, but it was empty. 'Herc?' she hissed. The main street was empty too. She waited a while, straining to see through the windows of the Mending House, but there was nothing. She hastened through the town, peering into alcoves and over fences, until she reached the bottom of the hill that led to St Halibut's. The path wound into darkness. Had he gone home?

'Herc?'

She began to climb, urgently, her breath coming in fast gulps, tripping over tussocks of grass strewn across the path. St Halibut's loomed ahead, its windows black. It had never looked so completely empty. She ran the last few steps across the driveway, through the door.

'Herc?' No answer.

Then she heard it. A rasping, high whistle, rhythmic, like a weak pair of bellows, coming from the kitchen.

And it was there that she found the Mended girl, sprawled on the floor, lips blue, gasping out what sounded like her last breaths in this world.

Chapter Twenty-Five

Nellie and Cuthbert stepped out from the kitchen on to the main factory floor, which looked like the result of a spaghetti bomb, threads trailing everywhere. Nellie tripped over something – another sleeping guard.

'This is weird,' Cuthbert whispered. 'Shouldn't the night guards be, y'know . . . awake?'

Nellie nodded distractedly. This was easy. Far too easy, in fact. But she wasn't one to say no to a freebie.

There was a cough from somewhere nearby.

'This way,' she said. 'Must be the dormitory.'

They walked through the door into another large, dark hall. Threadbare mats were spread on the floor in rows, each one with a Mended child on top of it, shivering, spluttering, dozing.

Except for one, which had Stef sitting upon it, looking gloomy. He jumped up on seeing them, and stared, as

though struggling to believe they were really there.

'What are you two doing here? Have you been sent for Mending?'

'We've come to rescue you,' Cuthbert said. 'Although that's turning out to be easier than we thought. It's a bit of luck those guards are so sleepy. And the door's not even locked.'

'I know. I unlocked it. But I couldn't leave, not without them.' He gestured at the sleeping bodies. 'It's no use. They won't get up. It's like they've had all the hope sucked out of them.'

Nellie glanced at them. 'Well, that's their lookout, innit? Get a shift on, can't you? Tig can't keep the Guvnor occupied forever.'

'Tig? She's here?'

'Yeah, course! Arfur told her to run off, but she said she wasn't going anywhere without you.'

'She said that?' Despite the situation, a flicker of pleasure warmed him.

'Yes! So get moving!'

But he looked away. 'I can't leave them. Ashna was meant to be helping us all escape, but our plan's gone wrong because Myers sent her out on a burglary instead.'

Nellie wrinkled her nose. Whoever Ashna was, they weren't going to wait around for her. Clearly, Stef was already half Mended and needed a kick up the behind.

'Well, *your* plan might have gone wrong, but I'm blowed if ours will. Cuth, help me drag him, will you? He's coming out of here whether he likes it or not.'

But Stef remained, stubborn, and Nellie and Cuthbert couldn't shift him.

'If Tig wouldn't leave me, then she'll understand why I can't run away from *them*.' He nodded at the Mended. 'You should go back and tell her. You should all go while you still can. I'll be OK.'

They stared, dumbfounded.

There was the sound of a slamming door, and then the click of three locks turning, one by one.

Cuthbert glanced nervously at Nellie. 'Was that . . .'

Footsteps drew closer. They paused, and there was a thud and a groan, as a boot met the flesh of a sleeping guard.

'Get up, you fool,' said a sneering voice.

The Mended children in the dormitory stirred and tensed at the sound of the Guvnor's voice as he invaded their nightmares.

Buttly stumbled through the doorway, clutching the sides of his head like it might fall off. His trousers, beltless, fell to his ankles. He was followed immediately afterwards by the person who had shoved him.

‘Well, Miss Happyday is being *very* generous today, sending me so many new recruits! Don’t bother trying to run. I have secured the side entrance. Your friend’s distraction was rather obvious.’

Nellie glowered. ‘So. Ainderby Myers. Or should I say *Burton Coggles*?’

For the tiniest moment, his face slackened in shock. Then he turned to his hapless guard and handed him the belt and keys he had found on the kitchen floor.

‘You there . . . Buttly, get yourself dressed properly and set this lot to work immediately. Until the machines are repaired, they will spin and weave by hand, all day and all night, until their fingers are bloody stumps. Nothing to eat, nothing to drink, and they work in silence.’

‘It’s the middle of the night, Guv . . .’

‘Yes, thank you, speaking clock. Just do it.’

‘You wanna watch it, *Coggles*,’ Nellie shot back. ‘You treat people like that and you’ll have a rebellion on your hands.’

‘Rebellion! I hardly think so.’ Nevertheless, his eyes flicked suspiciously between Nellie, Cuthbert and Stef. ‘Guard, these wretches must not be allowed to infect the others. They need intensive Mending. Starting right now.’

Chapter Twenty-Six

It was a while before the Mended girl could even speak. Tig sat with her warily for several minutes while the girl's breathing slowly grew less noisy and her lips took on a healthier tone, though her face was covered with a sheen of sweat. Gradually, Tig's wariness eased. This girl might be Mended, but she was clearly in no condition to carry out Ainderby Myers' evil bidding, whatever that might be.

'Where's Herc?' she asked. Then, at the girl's blank look, 'My little brother. Did you see him on your way up? We were outside the Mending House and now I can't find him and I'm afraid he . . . he might be . . .'

The girl shook her head, tried to speak, failed.

'It's a big hill,' Tig acknowledged. 'If you're not used to it.'

'My lungs,' Ashna finally managed. 'They're not good. It's the cotton dust. I haven't seen your brother, I'm sorry.

From what you've said, one of the guards has probably captured him. He will be in the Mending House by now.'

Oh, Herc. Why would he never, ever listen to her? She should have known he wouldn't, though – it was her job to look after him, no matter how difficult he made it. And she'd failed. Again.

Slowly, with pauses to catch her breath, Ashna told Tig who she was, and how she and Stef had come up with a plan to escape with the Mended, but that Myers had sent her up here before they could complete it.

Tig felt a hot wave of shame and despair overtake her. Of course Stef would have tried to help the others. Of course he wouldn't just plan to slip out on his own, like she would have. She had blamed herself for pushing him to go down to St Cod's in the first place, had felt guilty because he wasn't as strong as her. Now she saw that it hadn't been weakness on his part, but bravery, and she should instead be blaming herself for underestimating him.

If she hadn't insisted on her own stupid plans, Ainderby Myers would probably have stayed in his quarters, eaten the drugged eggs, and fallen asleep like he was supposed to. And right now everyone, including her brother, would be safe. It was unbearable.

Ashna sighed, frustrated. 'Myers has such a hold

over the Mended. It's more than just hard work and not enough gruel – they fear him. As long as he's with them, they won't have the will to stand up for themselves. I'm afraid that on his own, Stef won't be able to, either . . .'

Tig swallowed. 'Well, he's not on his own anymore. I've just gone and got my brand-new friends Mended. And Herc too, by the looks of it.' She felt tears prick at her eyes but dashed them away angrily. Crying was a luxury she didn't deserve.

'Go on, get it all out,' said Arfur, appearing at the kitchen door. 'Have a good old blub. It's good for you. I did tell you, though. I mean, I literally said "Don't go down there"—'

'Oh, shut up, Arfur. Why are you even still here?' Tig snapped.

'Careful,' Ashna muttered. 'I've seen this guy at the Mending House before. He's a friend of Myers.'

Tig smashed her hand on the table so hard it hurt. 'I *knew* it! You filthy toad, Arfur – you gave us away, didn't you? Oh, I was such a mug to trust you!'

Arfur looked taken aback.

'No, I . . . I didn't tell him nuffink. All I ever do is tip him off about rich places that have too much stuff, so he can send someone to take it off their hands.'

Ashna was shaking her head at him disbelievingly. 'It's

more than that. I heard what you said to him. You owe him your *life*.'

Tig stood over him, hands on hips, her expression telling him he had precisely one second to tell the truth.

Arfur made a face like he was trying to squeeze a lemon between his teeth.

'OK, OK. When I told you how he got Mended, way back . . . I forgot to mention something. It was me that did the apple-stealing what he got accused of. We was friends as kids, but they thought it was him and I . . . I didn't want to be Mended so I didn't . . .'

He trailed off.

'You let him take the blame,' Tig said. 'You coward.'

Arfur looked miserable. 'I know. Always have been.'

'So that's why you work for him?' Ashna asked. 'You feel guilty?'

Tig doubted the con man even knew

what the word meant, so was astonished when he nodded. 'When he finally got out, he found me. Thought he was gonna kill me, but instead he made me forge some documents for him to start a new life, get a new job far away. Made me go with him.'

'*You* got him the Mending House job?' asked Tig incredulously.

'Not exactly. I . . . helped,' he said. 'He didn't want much for a while after that, and I met Maisie, got married, started to make a life for meself. But then he got greedier, started asking me to do things for him. Maisie didn't like that. But what could I do?'

'Say no?' suggested Tig brutally.

'This is Ainderby Myers we're talking about. He can make anyone's life impossible. Besides, it don't look like your friends find it easy to say no to you, do they?'

Tig was stung into silence, her cheeks hot.

'All right,' said Ashna, sensing it would be helpful to move on. 'So you were trying to make it up to him.'

'Except what I come to realize is, see, I can never make it right, and he knows it. That's why I . . . Well, in the end I sent them matrons that newspaper article, anonymous like. They never knew who it came from.'

Tig gasped. '*You* did?'

'Yeah. I thought they'd snitch on him to DEATH

and he'd get caught. Except they didn't, did they? I was waiting and waiting, thinking why's nothing happening – I didn't know then that the stupid whatsits had gone and blackmailed him with it. When I found out they was both gone, and he didn't even know yet, I was gonna try and slip in here and take back the evidence, get him some other way. But then I thought, hold your horses, Arfur, they've got a DEATH inspector coming. Now those inspectors are thorough, I said to meself, bound to come across that article with snooping through all the nooks and crannies like they do. And who better to find it? Job done. Except it weren't a DEATH inspector what turned up, it was Snepp. And then you went and blew all of our covers by sending your mate down there. You lot are in real danger now, because I've gone and messed things up.'

'Why didn't you just show that article to DEATH yourself?'

He looked shamefaced. 'Wanted to keep my name out of it. Since that day when I nicked the apple and lied about it, I've been waiting for the law to catch me up. I done a lot worse since then, for his sake, to make up for it. I don't want them looking too closely at me.' He closed his eyes as though in pain. 'It's my fault he's the way he is, isn't it? I'm just as bad. Worse, maybe. I spent so long trying to do the right thing by him, and then do the right thing by you lot too, but I got it all wrong. Maisie used to say I'd picked the wrong friend, but the truth is I never had any.'

Tig found, much to her surprise, that despite her anger, she felt pity for Arfur. 'He doesn't own you, you know,' she told him quietly. Her next sentence felt wrenched out of her. 'You did something terrible, but what happened afterwards . . . the way he is now . . . that's down to him. Not you.'

Arfur put his head in his hands. 'Thing is, he's so powerful now, no one can do a thing about him. Except DEATH, of course, and they love 'im.'

Ashna nodded slowly. 'There are rumours about the Mending House, I'm sure. But DEATH can overlook rumours.' Then she stopped, and a smile began to creep across her face. 'So . . . we'll just have to do something that's impossible to ignore.'

Chapter Twenty-Seven

The gate bell rang just as Myers was about to make things interesting. He ignored it. He wasn't going to take his eyes off these children until they were well and truly exhausted in mind and body. He had dismissed most of the guards without pay, having established that they were far too sleepy to be useful. Buttly, Jerkson and Donk had sobered up with the help of a horsewhip, and they had woken up all the children, shoving and bullying them to fix the broken spinning machines. The fires were stoked up high, so that the heat on the factory floor was stifling. Sweat was pouring off the Guvnor's own face even though he stood still – he wiped it on his shirtsleeve and felt perspiration immediately break out again. He could see now that he had been lax with the new boy, and the other two. He wasn't going to make the same mistake twice. It was time for a proper interrogation of all of them – one that would hurt.

Except that there were these constant interruptions. Like now, when Jerkson, or possibly Donk, was telling him that Maisie had a parcel for him, which simply had to be signed for personally, by him and no one else.

He left Donk, or possibly Buttly, with instructions to thump anyone who slacked, and stalked off to the gate in a festering sulk. He'd had it up to here with thieving matrons, unruly kids, interfering so-called 'superiors' at DEATH HQ and now Maisie with another one of her infernal parcels to sign for. He nearly snapped her head off when she thrust her clipboard and pencil through the bars.

'It's the middle of the night! What's so urgent that the guards can't sign for it?' Though he wasn't sure any of his muscle-bound guards could sign their names and, in reality, he would not actually want her to entrust them with anything meant for him – they'd lose it on the short walk from the gate. 'Do you think I don't have more important things to do? The last one was only stationery, for goodness' sake. I'm sure you could leave them in the safe box. I'm sick to death of you constantly coming at me with a pencil, woman.'

Maisie merely examined her chipped scarlet nail polish with a bored air. 'Believe me, there are plenty of other places I'd like to stick it. Take it up with your superiors if you don't like it – it's them what insist I have to get these things to you on time. Here, don't forget to take your copy of the signing sheet, love – got to keep that paperwork nice and tidy for Lady Crock or she'll give you a slap on the wrist.'

He glanced down at her sharply. If he wasn't mistaken, she was being disrespectful. He made a mental note to report her to DEATH again, so they'd take away some of those illicit treats he knew she hoarded. The sugar was clearly going to her head.

'Now, you listen to me, *postwoman*: Lady Crock and I have never so much as set eyes on each other, and she has never set foot in this place. She is not in charge around here. *I* am. You would do well to remember that.' He snatched the parcel and his copy of the signing sheet, and gave her a meaningful glare as he walked back to the main door.

'Oh! Nearly forgot,' called Maisie after him. 'Got something important to tell you.'

'I doubt it,' retorted Myers, but he returned to the gate.

'It's a message from St Halibut's.'

That got his attention.

'She says she's got something you want, and she's prepared to give it to you at last, in return for a truce.'

So. Miss Happyday *was* still trying to pull the strings. He *knew* that killer-goat story was nonsense. Though perhaps . . . it had been a coded message of some kind, from her? But what did it mean? And if she was still alive, then maybe Snepp was too. Perhaps she was holding him hostage. Maybe she'd even captured Ashna. Miss Lackspittle as well, for all he knew. Not that he cared about any of them anymore. The whole world had spun out of control and his head hurt. But if Miss Happyday was playing around like this, at least it was clear she wasn't on the verge of giving the evidence to DEATH. The only thing that mattered now was getting it back.

'Good. Tell her to come here and we can discuss it.'

Maisie shook her head. 'She says you got to come out and meet her where no one will see. The crossroads on the way to Lardidar Valley.'

He straightened. 'No, she must come here.'

Maisie shrugged. 'I'm not tramping all the way up there again to take another message. Besides, she was setting off just as I left. Got the impression that if you weren't there, she had someplace else to take it. DEATH HQ, I think she said. I'm sure they'd look after it for you, whatever it is.'

Myers stood, uncertain, as the snow began to fall again, settling upon his shoulders. He looked up the dark road, and shivered in his sweat-soaked shirt.

Maisie looked him up and down. 'You don't half look cold. What you want is a nice woolly scarf, if you'll be out and about.' She wrapped hers more snuggly around her neck, and smirked before turning to leave. 'Cotton's not all it's cracked up to be, eh?'

Chapter Twenty-Eight

It had been almost disappointingly easy for Herc to climb up the Mending House wall, via a helpful ridge of decorative stones sticking out in a pattern, along a flat section, and finally up on to the roof – hardly more challenging than navigating the crawl space in the eaves around St Halibut's attic. The hard thing had been persuading Pamela not to follow him. He had had to speak quite harshly to her before she would leave him alone. It wasn't that he wouldn't rather have had her with him – only he feared she was too fat for the chimney.

He needn't have worried – it was so wide that he had to brace against it with arms and legs stretched out like a starfish. Its inner walls were crumbling; sections of brick loosened under his fingers and shoes, and tumbled into the fireplace below. But soon he was down, jumping the last few feet and crawling out into the room. Feeling about on the mantelpiece, he found a lamp, and soon its

light let him look around. An armchair, a table with a whisky glass and a decanter on it and, of course, the vault.

He stroked the ID card round his neck sorrowfully. It had been his fault about the money. Not Pamela's. He had been stupid; she had just been hungry. There was nothing he could do about the destroyed newspaper article that was important in some way he did not quite understand, but right now he was going to put the other thing right. He was going to replace the money, and who better to get it from than the richest man in Sad Sack, Ainderby Myers?

Tig would never have agreed to this, of course, which was why he hadn't told her, instead slipping away while she argued with Myers. Her plan, while not a bad effort, was not a patch on Herc's, which, in his view, was the only one that had any chance of succeeding. He had got the idea from his cartoon friends, Max and Moritz – in one of their tricks, they put gunpowder in a man's pipe, and it had blown all his hair clean off. Ainderby Myers didn't smoke a pipe, but Herc had decided to blow up something else, instead: the lock on the Guvnor's vault.

People thought he never listened, but in fact he almost always did. He had listened when the guard was boasting at the gate one day that his job was to look after the vast treasure that belonged to Ainderby Myers, and that he had to stand outside the first-floor room at the south-east corner for hours in a row without ever going to the toilet, and that as a result his bladder was now the same size as a horse's. At the time, Herc had thought the most interesting thing about that conversation was the size of the man's bladder, but soon after, he realized it meant an even more interesting thing: that if he wanted to get into that room, he'd need to go through the chimney.

He had also listened in Powders 'n' Potions when Mr Brimstone had told him off, because some of those powders would go up like fireworks if mixed together and exposed to a spark. The very powders he now had in dozens of paper bags in his pocket.

Only it was proving more difficult than he had expected. He was being careful, using only tiny amounts of powder to test, first. But every time he set a match to one, it simply glowed and gave off pungent smoke of varying scents. He'd tried mixing a few, in different combinations, but there had been not even the tiniest bang. It seemed Mr Brimstone had been exaggerating.

Sighing, he sat back on his heels and eyed the huge vault, which took up a quarter of the room and reached to the ceiling. It didn't feel like he'd been in here *too* long, but he was always a poor judge of time when his mind was occupied. The wooden door on the other side of the room remained shut. No guard burst in. The silence was complete.

Maybe he was being too cautious. Maybe he should stop trying out combinations and just go for it – mix everything together, all of it, stuff it in the vault lock, and see what happened.

Yes, that seemed sensible.

Chapter Twenty-Nine

Ashna was short of breath by the time she reached the mansion in Lardidar Valley. Tig had been very unsure about Ashna's audacious new plan, and kept asking her if she was well enough to carry it out. She had insisted that she was, but the truth was her head was pounding, her ribs were sore, and pinpricks of light kept floating around at the corners of her vision. Arfur had dropped her as close as he dared in Maisie's post cart – Maisie had, as Arfur had predicted, immediately agreed to help, despite her ex-husband's involvement in the scheme; to save Ashna's lungs the walk, and because speed was of the essence. But the long driveway was gravelled, and the noise of Bernard's hooves and the wheels would have been enough to wake the dead, and so Ashna had hopped down and watched him depart back into the night before making her way across the grass instead.

Ashna cast an experienced eye over her target. The

architect had clearly been told to spare no expense on designing this mansion – it was flashy, with Roman-style columns and stone lions with their mouths open as though roaring loudly about how wealthy the owner was.

According to Arfur, the owner was all alone in there, in a bedroom on the top floor, at the other end of the mansion from the ground-floor window she was aiming for. The servants had their own quarters on the other side of the stables. There should be no problem.

She felt the familiar rush of adrenalin as she moved silently over the wet grass, eyes peeled for any movement. She had not asked to be a burglar, and she knew it was wrong to steal; she despised Myers for making her do it. The thrill was there all the same – the ever-present possibility of capture; the skill required to enter unobserved, remove the target and escape. And she was very, very good at it.

The three fingers and thumb of her right hand felt along the bottom of the large wooden sash-window frame. Just as Arfur had said, a small section was rotten and crumbling. She dug at it with her fingernails until they could slip between the sill and the frame, and applied pressure. It resisted, and then gave, sliding smoothly upwards. She allowed herself a small smile. Her niggling worry that Arfur might have given her

false information was unfounded.

Silently, she heaved her body up, threw her leg over the sill and sat astride it, half in, half out of the room.

At the very edge of her hearing, she caught a noise.

Barking.

Across the darkened park, a shape was approaching at speed.

Arfur had told her about the dog, too. A slavering, vicious creature that would not hesitate to sink its teeth into her throat and never let go. She must avoid it at all costs, he had told her. Get in fast.

Now that the guard dog was closer, she could see why.

It was huge. Its ears were pricked forward as it ran, its white teeth almost glowing against brown-and-black mottled fur. Its volley of enraged barks echoed around the brickwork.

She hastened inside, and yanked down on the big window.

Having slid up so easily, however, it was now stuck fast.

She grasped it with both hands and put all her weight on it; it did not budge.

The dog's mouth was open, tongue glistening. In seconds it would be upon her, through the window.

Desperately she shook the frame, hammered at the sides to loosen it.

The dog leaped.

The sash dropped.

Fur and teeth and claws met the glass with a yelp of pain and humiliation, and slid down, thumped heavily to the ground.

Ashna turned and immediately spotted her prize on a dressing table in the corner: a diamond necklace draped artfully over a cushion. With hands that were only slightly trembling, she grasped it.

The dog was snarling and howling its rage outside. There was no time to lose.

And then someone appeared at the inner door, in a dressing gown, holding a lantern aloft.

A shriek split the air.

'THIEF!'

Tig could see Myers sitting on the stone from some distance away – the clouds had cleared around the moon, and a milky light bathed the crossroads. She looked past him, where the road ran in a straight line out towards Lardidar Valley. It was dark and silent. Nobody in their right mind would travel down it at this time of night, except robbers and murderers.

And her.

It hadn't felt great to have someone else come up with a grand plan and give her a dangerous job to do, but she had to admit, this one might actually work. And somewhere inside her, there was the tiniest relief, like a muscle relaxing; she didn't have to be on top of everything – there were others on her team now.

Arfur had been nervous, though. 'But will it be enough? Gotta get him all sewn up tight, or he'll make sure we never get another chance.'

Tig had marvelled at Arfur's 'we'. Whatever demons

he had been wrestling with, he seemed to have finally picked a side. Unless, of course, it was a trick. She'd find out shortly, in any case.

In the dim light of the kitchen as they'd cooked up their final, last-ditch scheme, she had realized something: the burden of figuring things out and making decisions was not hers alone, and it never had been. Stef, Nellie, Cuthbert, even her brother – who *still* hadn't turned up, and so must be in the Mending House too – would be cooking something up at their end, she felt sure. But it would be hard for them to do anything unless they could get the Guvnor out of the building . . . somehow.

Which was why she was here.

Tig took a deep, shaky breath, and forced her steps onwards. When she was close enough to see the steam of his breath, she stopped, and put her hand in her flapping coat, as though for a piece of paper.

'So it's you again, the *protestor.* What am I doing here, girl?' he barked. 'Where is Miss Happyday?'

'She sent me.' Tig glanced down the road behind him. 'I've got the evidence.'

He was walking stiffly towards her, his skin almost blue with the cold.

'Expecting someone else to join you?' he asked, following her gaze. 'We seem to be all alone.'

There was a vicious glint in his eye, a horrible look of triumph. Tig stepped back, all her delaying tactics having fled her mind. The road to Lardidar Valley lay stubbornly empty. No one was coming.

She had arrived too early. Or something had happened to Ashna. How long had he been there, waiting for her? Her blood chilled. Had he already met Ashna on the road and—

A rustle at her ear. He was next to her, his breath on her cheek. 'Do you really expect me to believe Miss Happyday would send a young girl on her own with such a precious paper? And what about my money? You have *nothing*. She has wasted my time yet again, and it ends now.'

Tig took another step back. 'If you just wait a moment . . . payment is coming.' She just needed to stall him. If they went slowly enough, it might give Ashna the time she needed. 'Let's start walking to St Halibut's and Miss Happyday can explain.'

His hand was on her shoulder, bringing her to a halt, his fingers digging into the skin. 'Oh, I don't think so. You won't be coming.'

Chapter Thirty

Buttly was complaining of a headache, while Jerkson was holding his hands over his ears. Donk had most of the contents of the large saucepan of gruel down his uniform and was scrubbing furiously at it in the kitchen. The three guards had been left alone in a situation that none of their training had prepared them for: supervising unMended children. They were frankly out of their depth.

The new children had started playing up the moment the Guvnor had left, wandering in and out of the dormitory and the machine room, circling like vultures. The guards had lasted ten minutes before giving in to their incessant demands for food – the children had claimed they couldn't possibly do any work on empty bellies. They'd been asking for more and more outlandish things, all talking at once, and the Mended children had begun watching this strange turn of events with interest.

Jerkson had made an excuse about needing the toilet and disappeared for twenty minutes, but now that he was back, things had got worse rather than better. Myers must have been gone for at least an hour now, and the guards had decided that, rather than make another pot of gruel or try to get anyone to work, they should just get everyone into bed until the Guvnor returned.

Now the new children had spilt gruel over their own clothes and faces, and were flicking it at each other, sniggering. One or two of the Mended were joining in, hesitantly at first and then with more gusto. Someone had tipped a load of it into the boiler, and the fire had gone out. Donk had tripped over Nellie's outstretched foot, resulting in the saucepan accident.

Jerkson was getting jumpy. 'Buttly, I don't like the way they're looking at me. Even the Mended ones are starting to act weirdly, and they're whispering every time my back's turned.'

'Don't turn your back on them, then,' replied Buttly, who'd been in the army, and so knew a thing or two about combat. He was trying not to blink; these kids seemed to be in a different position every time he did.

'They keep moving!' Jerkson wasn't even sure how many of them there were anymore; it was like trying to count a bucketful of eels.

'You didn't wash your hands, did you, my good man?' Cuthbert said, frightening the life out of Jerkson by popping up suddenly and grasping his wrists. 'Did you know that underneath your fingernails, you pick up things like worm eggs, which you can't even see, and then if you put your fingers in your mouth or your nose, they go in and then they hatch and eat you from the inside.'

Horrified, Jerkson began to make for the door, but Buttly grabbed his arm. 'Oi, where d'you think you're going? You're not leaving me on me own, mate.'

'I don't want worms,' Jerkson hissed. 'Anyway, you'll be fine – it's only kids, innit? You're a grown man.'

'And you're what, a baby mouse? *You* get them into bed, if it's that easy. Or Donk can,' he added as the other guard came back in, soaked to the skin.

'Hmm,' said Donk, in a distracted tone that suggested he wasn't available to hear his fellow guards' concerns right now, but that they could leave a message. He spotted Nellie in a corner, fervently whispering into a Mended boy's ear. ''Ere, what you saying? Get away from him.'

She looked Donk square in the eye. 'Nah.'

Donk had not encountered this sort of thing in the Mending House before.

The boy Nellie had been whispering to blinked slowly, as though strange thoughts were trickling through his mind. 'No?' he said, very quietly, and then jumped and looked around, shocked by his own voice.

'Stop that!' said Donk, poking a finger at her. 'That's enough.'

'I was just saying,' said Nellie, 'that I don't fancy gruel.'

'Me neither,' added Stef, from the other side of the dorm. 'You know what my friend Herc would say we should have? Cake.'

'Oh, yes,' agreed Cuthbert. 'A nice bit of chocolate cake. That would be just the ticket.'

Buttly massaged his temple vigorously. 'We don't have no cake, kid. We don't even have gruel no more, since you lot decorated this place with it.' He beckoned Donk over and hissed in his ear. 'We should have clocked off ages ago. Are we getting paid overtime?'

Donk shrugged sadly. 'What do you think? Can't go nowhere till the Guvnor comes back, though.'

'But the Guvnor isn't here, is he?' said Stef loudly, announcing it to the room. 'Perhaps he'll never come back.'

The ripples from his words seemed to spread through

the dorm. The Mended seemed to straighten, grow taller at the thought.

'I think . . .' whispered a pale girl with wispy blonde hair. 'I think I would like some cake.'

The boy next to her began to smile, on and off, as though the muscles had forgotten exactly how to do it. 'Yes . . . I remember cake. Sponge cake. We used to get it under the counter at Ma Yeasty's when the shop was closed.'

'With icing,' came another voice, laced with excitement.

'Chocolate icing!'

'Marshmallows!'

'Marsh-flippin'-mallows?' yelled Buttly, panic-stricken. 'This is a DEATH Mending House! We don't have no illegal drugs in here. For the last time: we don't have no bouncy castles, we don't play hide-and-seek, and we don't have no cake. AND. ZERO. MARSH. MALLOWS!'

Cuthbert frowned. 'Well, I shall certainly be making a complaint. These guards need retraining.'

Nellie smirked. 'Guards? Is that what they are? I thought they was clowns.'

Buttly's trousers, still missing their belt, slipped downwards at that moment, with perfect timing. A loud guffaw from somewhere in the corner set all the children off like a line of helpless dominoes, shoulders shaking, eyes streaming.

'Oi!' shouted Buttly, red-faced over the noise. 'You're for it when the Guv gets back, you cheeky little twerps!'

Nellie smiled sweetly at him.

'Us? We're just getting started.'

Chapter Thirty-One

Myers did not notice the crunching noise behind until it was almost upon him. He whirled around and found that he had to leap out of the way of an ornate carriage that thundered to a halt barely a hair's breadth away, pulled up by a red-and-gold-liveried footman. Four horses snorted and tossed their heads, blasting steam from their nostrils into his face. He dropped Tig, and she fell to the ground, clutching her throat and gasping in great gulps of air.

An occupant of the reckless carriage popped her head out of the window, an elderly woman with white hair under a scarlet beret. 'Is that poor girl all right? It looks awfully like—'

Myers rounded on her with the fury of someone who has been severely inconvenienced all day and would very much like to be left alone to commit murder without any further interruptions. 'You nitwit! You nearly killed

me!' He wagged a finger at the driver, who was looking down his nose from his high seat, sneering. 'I'll have you prosecuted for dangerous driving,' he yelled.

Somebody opened the door on the other side of the carriage and got out. When he saw who it was he was furious. His burglar. 'You! I gave you one simple task! And now I find you gallivanting about the country in a carriage!'

Ashna blinked at him innocently. 'I was just doing my job, like you told me to.'

The elderly lady cleared her throat. 'If I might venture an opinion—'

'Shut it,' he snapped at her. 'Nobody asked you, you old trout. I am talking to my employee here, so mind your own beeswax.'

At this, the woman's eyes narrowed. 'Oh, she works for you, does she?'

'Yes,' he snarled. 'And I don't know what she was doing in your carriage, but she's my property, so you can toddle off back to wherever you came from and keep your mouth shut. I can make life very difficult for you, so—'

'Can you, indeed? I should very much like to know how.'

He laughed. 'My name is *Ainderby Myers.* I assume you have heard of me? If so, you'll know what I can do.' He waited for her reaction. It was not quite what he expected.

She drew herself up straighter on her seat. '*My* name is Lady Crock.'

Every muscle in Myers' face grew slack. Of all possible moments to meet his boss for the first time, this had to be up there with the worst. He swayed forward, then back. 'Urghh,' he said. 'Urgghhh . . .'

'Quite. Perhaps you can explain why I found your employee inside my home, trying to steal my diamond necklace.'

Myers' eyes flicked to Ashna and back. 'I . . . I . . .'

'She told me it was on your orders, but I found that hard to believe. However, I see now that it is true.'

Myers finally found his voice. 'Please! No, it is not! My dear lady—'

Lady Crock tutted. 'Don't you "dear lady" me, Myers, or I'll have my driver kick your impertinent backside into the middle of next week. And don't insult me by pretending ignorance when you have already confessed that you gave her the orders. She is clearly one of your Mended.'

'Yes, but . . .' he stuttered. 'No, she . . . she was meant to be somewhere else! If she has tried to burgle you it is not on my authority! Surely you cannot think I would—'

She talked over him. 'I see. It's all just a coincidence, is it?' Her tone dared him to keep on with this. 'To bring your criminal activities to *my* door . . . The nerve! Pierson,' she addressed the liveried driver. 'Escort Mr Myers to a seat.'

'Lady Crock! I assure you—'

'Your Mended burglar can walk back with that other girl, who I suppose is another of your unfortunate charges. You and I need to have a private chat, Mr Myers.'

Pierson slipped down from his seat, approached Myers, and with the utmost politeness guided him towards the carriage so his feet did not touch the ground.

Doors were slammed, whips cracked, and the carriage was soon a disappearing dot on the road ahead.

'Took your time, didn't you?' said Tig as Ashna helped her to her feet.

Ashna grinned. 'Hey, I can't help it if I'm such a good burglar – it's hard to get caught. Luckily Arfur was right about the dog. Noisy thing.'

Tig grinned. 'Arfur's still a slippery little liar, but turns out he's *our* slippery little liar.'

Chapter Thirty-Two

'Donk! Buttly! Jerkson!'

The Guvnor rattled the iron gate in his fists. There was no reply. No sign of any of his useless guards.

He was fast moving through shock and entering full-blown panic. The carriage journey with his incensed boss had been one of the most unpleasant experiences of his life. It had proved almost impossible to figure out how he was going to wriggle out of this mess while she was so relentlessly tearing strips off him. What made it worse was that he could hear the driver chuckling to himself up front while she was shouting at him.

'I can't imagine where they are,' he blustered now.

Lady Crock turned her cold scrutiny on him. He could tell she still hadn't forgiven him for calling her an old trout. 'I must say, if this is an example of how you run the Mending House, I have grave concerns about your suitability for the post.'

'What? No! You'll see, you'll see.' He fumbled in a pocket, dropped something and banged his head on the gate as he picked it up. 'I have my key, here we are.'

On entering his quarters, he immediately set about lighting candles and a lantern on the desk, partly to still his shaking hands, and partly to give him time to think things through. Why had his burglar been at Lady Crock's house, of all places, when she was supposed to be at St Halibut's, stealing back the evidence against him? Was Miss Happyday behind it somehow? Had she turned his own burglar against him? And what on earth had she done with Snepp? He would never have thought her so cunning.

'Would you like a drink, to warm you after such a cold journey? I can get a guard to make some tea.' He fussed about, plumping up the cushion on his chair for her, brushing a speck of dust from it while she cast her eye disapprovingly over the mess of papers on his desk. 'Then we can clear up this entire misunderstanding.'

There was a loud knock and Buttly's voice came from the other side. 'Guv, Guv!'

'Not now!' he roared.

'I do not need tea, Myers,' Lady Crock said abruptly. 'But explain this.' She plucked a paper from his desk and held it up.

I, Ainderby Myers, do hereby certify that I have received advance payment of one thousand pounds, in exchange for the diamond necklace currently in the possession of Lady Crock, which I shall acquire by secret means.

Myers' eyes were goggling. His finger was pointing at the paper, his cheeks aflame. 'What the . . . that is not . . . Lady Crock, you must see that I would never have written that! It's not my handwriting.'

'But it is undoubtedly your signature.'

Ainderby Myers

He craned over it. There was no denying it. He had spent years perfecting his ornate scribble, believing that a man's stature and worth could be ascertained by how many scrolls and curlicues he could fit into his first name; it had the extra benefit of being unforgettable.

'That's my signature, but I didn't sign it.' He was blinking rapidly, as though his eyeballs had malfunctioned.

'Oh, well, that's perfectly clear,' she drawled, letting it drop to the desk.

'Guv!' came Buttly's voice again, with some urgency.

'Not *now*, man! Lady Crock, can't you see? It's a trick! Someone has played a . . .' He whirled around as though the person who had done it might be laughing at him from the corner of the room. 'It makes no sense! Why would I sign such a paper? It would incriminate me!'

'Indeed it would.' She raised an eyebrow meaningfully at him.

His hands bent into claws and he clutched at his head. 'Who could have done this?' At once, a light dawned. 'Maisie . . .' he whispered. 'I signed for a parcel . . .'

'What are you blathering about, man?' Lady Crock was fast losing her patience. 'I am beginning to think you have entirely lost control, not only of this establishment but your mind.'

'The postwoman, of course! She must be a criminal

mastermind! She's behind all of this!' He gasped. 'And she's in league with the matron!'

'The *postwoman?*' repeated Lady Crock icily.

'Guv!' Buttly was now hammering on the door with the desperation of a man who has had six cups of tea and now finds the toilet engaged by someone who has settled in with the newspaper.

'I am close to discovering what is going on,' Myers was saying, almost to himself. There was a strange, fevered light in his eyes. 'The Mended . . . they may have seen something. They will not deny me the truth. I shall have it out of them.' He grabbed the lantern, pushed past Buttly and entered the factory floor just as the dormitory door on the other side of the room burst open, and Donk appeared momentarily in it, eyes bulging like a couple of eggs being squeezed out of a chicken.

'Help—' he managed, before he was overwhelmed by a flow of the Mended pouring over him, flattening him under their feet. They were not the Mended as Myers had left them. They were chanting, but not the brainwashed chants he had taught them. These were . . . ruder. The tide of shouting, running, laughing merged into a riotous noise through which nothing else could be heard.

Lady Crock's mouth was moving, her chin juddering in outrage as her lips formed questions he could not hear, let alone answer. The Mended were flowing around him now, and he felt himself shoved this way and that, pinched and tickled and jostled.

He began to flail about, trying to catch his assailants but missing them by millimetres.

Thwump!

OM!

A tremendous explosion made his ears ring, and for a second he thought it was his own temper erupting from his brain. But then a shockwave swept through the room, and the glass in every window of the Mending House shattered outwards.

Everyone froze in position, ducked low. Silence fell. Then the world began again. The Mended continued their exodus, throwing blankets over jagged window sills, climbing out.

The source of the explosion was the floor above.

Myers sprinted upstairs, leaping three steps at a time, barely aware of Lady Crock following as she screeched instructions at confused guards behind him, ordering them to arrest him.

There was only one thing that mattered now: his vault, and in it, the last remaining hope for his future.

Chapter Thirty-Three

Tig and Ashna had arrived at the gates just as the force of the explosion blew them right open, the brass bell pinging off and landing halfway across the street.

The Mended, free, flowed through and then stopped, uncertain, in front of them. Nellie pushed her way through.

'Better late than never!' she said, seeing the others. 'Where've you been?'

Cuthbert and Stef joined her, panting. Tig threw her arms around Stef, and he patted her shoulders awkwardly. 'I'm so sorry, Stef,' she said, muffled, into his chest.

But he was looking around,

over their heads. 'What happened? Where's Herc?'

Tig went cold. 'He's not with you?'

He swallowed. 'I thought he was with you . . .'

'Oi,' Nellie interrupted. 'I think we need to move the Mended away from here. They're getting scared.'

It was true. The initial elation that had driven the children from their prison had ebbed away as soon as they were beyond its gates. They were staring around warily, clutching each other.

'Take them up to St Halibut's,' said Tig firmly. 'I've got to find Herc.'

Stef nodded, and turned to go back through the gates. 'I'm coming with you.'

There was a ring of black around a large hole in the wall of the Mending House, where the explosion must have come from. Without the need for any discussion, the two friends headed for it.

The upper floor of the Mending House was awash with notes, coins and jewellery, scattered on the floorboards. There was an acrid smell of burning, and smoke hung in the air. Lady Crock and a couple of guards were standing next to what had once been a large vault but was now a pile of twisted metal. They were keeping their distance from the gaping hole in the wall, through which much

of Sad Sack could now be seen. Ainderby Myers was frantically filling his pockets with coins and precious stones, not that it could do him any good now.

'Oh no,' said Tig. This had all the hallmarks of one of Herc's experiments.

'Do not come in here,' Lady Crock commanded, on seeing them. 'Health and safety regulations three to fifty-six point nine have been well and truly broken.'

'I think my brother was in there!' Tig sobbed.

Stef pushed past Lady Crock and scoured the room. The walls were blackened, the ceiling crumbling. An armchair was fried to a crisp in the corner, only its frame and scraps of cloth remaining. There was a pile of ash behind it. Stef knelt carefully and picked something up from it. It was a charred piece of plastic.

'That's the inspector's ID card,' Tig whispered. 'Herc was wearing it . . .'

'Well, thank goodness for that!' Herc cried, squeezing past them both and snatching it from Stef's grasp. 'It must have fallen off when I ran on to the landing. The chain's busted.' His face fell. 'It's ruined! You can't even see the grinning skull logo anymore—' He stopped as Tig hugged the breath from him.

'Herc! We thought you were . . .'

'A hero!' He nodded. 'Yes, I am. My plan seems to have done the trick.'

'*Your* plan? That nearly blasted us all to smithereens,' objected Tig. '*My* plan, you mean. Well, mine and Ashna's.' Then she flushed. 'Except, I think Stef might have had something to do with it too.'

Stef made a non-committal noise. 'Looks like we all messed up our plans, separately, but somehow our mess-ups combined, have messed up the Guvnor more.'

Herc rolled his eyes. 'Oh, yes, *everyone* has to take the credit as usual. Just remember: there's only one person in this room who actually *blew things up*.' He twisted round in Tig's arms and frowned up at her. 'Is Pamela all right? I had to leave her behind.'

'Pamela? Has a child been left unattended?' asked Lady Crock sharply. In their relief, they had entirely forgotten the DEATH official was there.

'Our mother,' said Tig, just as Herc said, 'Our goat.'

'Our mother's goat,' explained Stef quickly. 'On our farm. Where we live,' he added. 'With our mother, who is also alive. Because we're not orphans. Never have been. And when Herc talked about blowing things up just now, he was referring to . . . uh . . .'

'Balloons,' supplied Tig.

'Because it's my birthday,' agreed Herc, beaming.

If Lady Crock found this unconvincing, she clearly had other fish to fry. She drew a large file from her briefcase. 'All present and correct, then,' she said. 'Apart from the small matter of the *entire* cohort of Mended children.' She pursed her lips. 'And this really takes the biscuit – a horde of clearly stolen treasures in the Mending House! I have authority here,' she told the guards. 'Restrain this man. He is a criminal.'

Buttly nodded. 'OK. But, just to be clear, who?' he asked.

They all looked around. Myers was gone.

Chapter Thirty-Four

The smoke had been quite thick in the vault room, and the others far too preoccupied to notice that Ainderby Myers had crawled to the fireplace, pockets bulging with as many of his stolen riches as he could stuff into them.

The explosion had loosened many of the chimney's bricks, and once or twice he put his weight on to one that collapsed beneath his foot as he clambered up inside, leaving him hanging by his fingernails, shoes scrabbling against the sides. But this was his only chance, and he gave it his all.

By the time his numb fingers curled around the top edge of the chimney, and his arms pulled his exhausted, soot-covered body into the clean air of the roof, he was almost spent. He lay panting, and coughing, his eyes gummed up by sticky dust. He ripped off his shirt and turned it inside out to wipe his lashes, then, corneas

stinging, blinked through his blurry vision.

What he saw made no sense.

In front of his nose, on the roof tiles, were a pair of very hairy white legs, wearing some kind of tiny, dainty shoes.

He rubbed his eyes again. Not shoes; hooves.

The legs were hairy, and led up to a deep chest, at the top of which was a long face. Presumably behind all this was the rest of a body, but he could not remove his gaze from the eyes, once it had fastened upon them. Never before had he seen eyes that understood everything he felt. The creature seemed, to him, to truly get it: the hatred, the betrayal, the disgust at humankind. Because it felt the same.

It must be a vision, he thought, shaking his throbbing head. His ears were still ringing from the explosion, his lungs ached, his arms and legs were sore and scratched from slipping and sliding up the chimney. But he was free. The roof of St Cod's was a mere leap away, and from there a stealthy journey from rooftop to rooftop, and finally down to the long road that led to the coast.

Some seaside Mending House, perhaps. A place far away where he could start over. Again.

He drew strength from the mystical goat conjured up by his imagination, which he was sure had appeared to encourage him on his way. He groaned with effort and dragged himself to his feet, stumbling a little, grasping the goat's coarse hair for balance.

It felt quite real.

Meeehhhhh, said the goat.

All the hairs on its back rose into a ridge, and its head dipped, though it kept its eyes on him. Its horns glimmered in the moonlight.

Those eyes. He got the distinct impression that the creature had been expecting someone else to come up the chimney, and that it was not exactly thrilled at his presence.

Something that someone had said, not long ago, floated across his memory. *Killed by a goat . . . a really, really cross one.*

Its lips drew back, revealing a set of yellow teeth in its lower jaw, and hard pink gums at the top. It was inexplicably horrifying.

He wavered a little on his feet and took a step back.

'No . . . you and me . . . we're the same,' he gasped.

ME-E-E-HH! The goat reared up on its hind legs.

Myers took another step back. And walked into thin air.

Epilogue

Two months later

Today had been inspection day at St Halibut's. DEATH had sent their top inspector.

He'd seen the children – all forty or so of them. He'd seen the house. He'd seen what they'd been up to lately.

Most importantly, he was now leaving in just as good health as when he had arrived. This, Tig felt, was definitely progress.

She followed him down the step by the front door and out on to the drive. 'How did we do?' she asked, nervously. 'What will you say in your report?'

The inspector breathed in the clean air of the hilltop, and let the sun warm his face. He sucked his teeth. 'Lemme see. The place is filthy, your grammar sucks, you've done nothing but run about and make a mess of the place, far as I can see.' He nodded. 'I like it.'

Tig gave him a warning look. 'Arfur, that is *not* what you're going to write.'

He dug her in the ribs and chuckled. 'Course not.' He put on a clipped accent: '"The children of St Halibut's are perfect in every way; their academic standards are top-notch, as is their behaviour and their housekeeping. Miss Happyday rules with great wisdom and rectitude."' He winked at her. 'I'll put a semicolon in there somewhere. They love those.'

The good thing about DEATH inspecting, according to Arfur, was that it didn't take up much of his time, which left him free to do what he winkingly called 'bit of this, bit of that'.

Tig marvelled at him – a man who could make even semicolons sound dodgy. 'I can't understand how they made you an inspector. How on earth did you swing it?'

'Lady Crock gave me a lovely reference.'

Of course she had. In the aftermath of the explosion, Lady Crock had been terribly worried – all this chaos made her look very bad. Dreadful that such a thing could have been going on right under her nose . . .

Luckily, Arfur had appeared at her elbow at just the right moment, explaining how he was just the man to fix up this mess for her, if she would give him a few days and a large amount of money. *Her* bosses would never need to hear about what had happened, he promised.

Years of practice selling dodgy knick-knacks had

taught him a thing or two about persuasion, and she had been unable to refuse his special trustworthy smile.

And for once, Arfur was true to his word – within two days, the Mending House was patched back up, looking as good as new, and all the neighbours paid off enough so that they couldn't remember anything about an explosion, or a bunch of Mended children escaping, *or* a dodgy Guvnor who'd mysteriously disappeared.

When Lady Crock returned and saw what had been done, her delight and relief knew no bounds.

'You're wasted as a salesman. I wish you would come and work for me,' she had said. 'I need a new governor I can trust. Will you consider it?'

He refused, however. Having avoided the Mending House once, he wasn't about to live there voluntarily. 'Tell you what, though, I know someone who'd be good. I'll ask.'

'Very well. But what will *you* do? Do you have any qualifications? I should like to recommend you for a DEATH career.'

'Funny you should ask,' he said, and brought out his Certificate of Inspectoring (first-class distinction with highly commended honours), which was definitely not forged and certainly not printed on stolen Inspectors' Guild headed notepaper. 'This sort of thing, you mean?'

★

Up at St Halibut's, it took a while for the victims of Ainderby Myers to properly unMend. Many of them were ill. Some of them would suffer with their lungs for the rest of their lives, but here there was always someone around to rub their backs when they coughed, and fetch things for them when they were too tired to move.

And once their minds were clear – free from Myers' influence and the exhaustion of heavy work – they kept wanting to learn things. Starved of the opportunity for so long, they demanded books, and pestered Tig, Stef and even Herc, until they explained how the vegetables grew, and how to tell the time, and how to make a birthday cake. Their desire for knowledge was catching, and soon Ashna, Tig, Stef, Cuthbert, Nellie and even Herc began to hold little classes, spreading the teaching between them. They did not go so far as to dig up the buried textbooks, but they could often be found nosing through the mobile library that Arfur set up on Maisie's old post cart, finding paperbacks and comics that caught their interest, and bringing them home to share. There were no spelling tests, though: on this Herc was firm. After Nellie's classes, a large number of the Mended knew how to pick pockets.

Stef had expected the newly unMended children to look up to his friends – and they did – but to his surprise they sought him out especially. They looked to him for things that he hadn't realized he was good at – comforting the little ones when they fell, bandaging their grazed knees, helping them keep calm when they struggled for breath, reading with them, playing tickle monster. The older ones confided in him, because he always listened, and sat with them while they cried for friends they'd lost.

Wayward children were still being sent to the Mending House, but they were no longer spinning cotton. Instead they were knitting, under Maisie's indulgent eye. She and her new Mended staff kept perfect records, which was enough to keep Lady Crock happy, and they were producing a very large number of jumpers, cardigans and scarves, which meant they made a tidy profit. Of course, it helped that the young workers were fuelled by vast quantities of Ma Yeasty's pastries and loaves, though they still couldn't get her to wash her hands. After a hard day's knitting and purling, the Mended could often be seen in the yard of the Mending House, playing football with what looked suspiciously like a broccoli muffin.

Ainderby Myers had disappeared without trace. Some said he had been captured and sent to prison. Others said he had escaped justice, forged himself a new identity and was running a Mending House under another name, far away, in some other isolated spot. Still others reckoned he had perished after falling from the roof of the Mending

House, though no body was ever found – the clear-up had been so hasty that it might have been missed.

A rumour started that the Mending House was haunted. One night, around a bonfire while they toasted marshmallows on sticks, Nellie entertained the children with spooky stories of a strange, spindly, cotton-suited figure that could be seen during a full moon, stalking the rooftop, searching for his treasure.

Herc cuddled up closer to Pamela, burying his nose in her stiff white hair. He had been hurt at first, that she had disappeared that night, and not turned up back home till late, by which time he was beside himself with anxiety; he worried he had insulted her by insisting on climbing the roof alone. But now, with all this talk of ghosts, he was glad that she had kept well out of it.

Tig took Nellie aside and admonished her. 'Why are you making stuff like that up? You'll scare them!'

'Oh, they love it,' Nellie retorted. 'Besides, blame Mr Brimstone – it was him that started it. You know how he lives opposite the Mending House? Before Arfur shut him up with some money, he was going on about how he'd seen a ghost that night, on the roof. A white one, with horns.'

'Daft old fool. He must've been nibbling some of his dodgy herbs. A ghost, with horns?'

'Yeah. I *think* that's what he said.'

THE END

Acknowledgements

The Orphans of St Halibut's was made into a book because of a lot of people who aren't me. I owe them more than I can ever repay, so they'll have to make do with my heartfelt thanks instead:

Firstly, my mum and dad, Jenny and Ken Wills – for everything. I wish you were still here so that you could embarrass me in bookshops just as you threatened. I should have written more quickly. But I know I was very lucky to have you as long as I did.

Kate Shaw, for her enthusiasm, commitment, patience, wisdom and endless hard work on my behalf.

David Tazzyman, for saying 'yes' and making St Halibut's come alive with his incredible skill.

Lucy Pearse and Cate Augustin, my editors at Macmillan, for understanding where I was trying to go with the book and guiding me there. Susila Baybars, for copy-editing and Nick de Somogyi for proofreading. And everyone else involved in the process, including Sarah Clarke, Ella Chapman, Jo Hardacre, Emma Quick, Rachel Vale, Tracey Ridgewell, Charlotte Parker, Eve Roberts, and Laura Carter. You are all my heroes.

Special thanks to Tiggy and to Ashna, for the loan of your names. Do I have to give them back now?

Apologies to the people of Ainderby Miers in Yorkshire, both for naming a villain after your town and then adding insult to injury by changing the spelling.

My writing friends and critique group partners, especially the Swaggers, without whom I would have been very lonely. Thanks for the laughing emojis even when my jokes didn't deserve them. You're all inspirational – and kind, which is even more important.

And lastly, the very best people of all – my husband, Rob, and my children, Fraser and Cameron. Without your support, I'd never have got as far as the first word.

Turn the page for an exclusive extract
from the next hilarious adventure

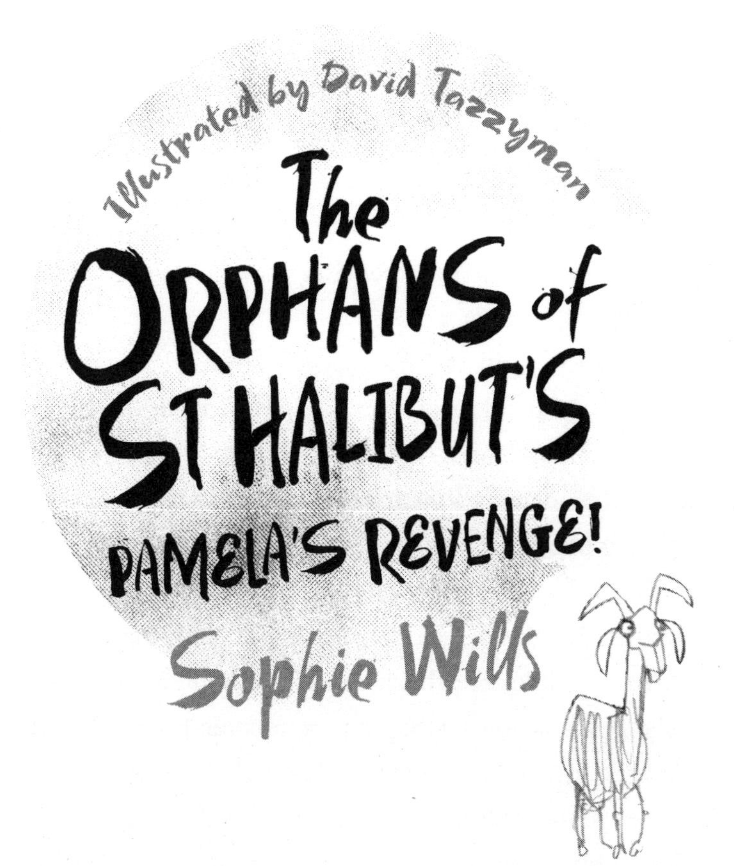

Chapter One

'The whole point of Miss Happyday being dead,' said Herc, 'is that we don't have to do this sort of thing anymore.'

His sister's grip did not slacken as she dragged him down the steep hill away from St Halibut's Home for Waifs and Strays. Sometimes he felt she could be a lot like their not-so-dear departed matron, especially when it came to stopping him from doing what he wanted.

Herc's latest marshmallow recipe had produced a fantastically glossy, thick, pale liquid and turned the kitchen air into breathable treacle; the ultimate sweet, fluffy treat was now cooling on the counter. He'd only just managed to pour it out before Tig had stormed into the kitchen yelling that they were going to be late, that all the other orphans were down at the Festival already, and if he didn't come right NOW there would be consequences. She didn't say what *kind* of consequences, but over the eight long years of his life, he had learned that if you were promised them, they were never good.

It was particularly unfair that he had been forced to abandon his marshmallows to go to the Sad Sack Festival, an event so dangerously dull that it had actually killed one of Arfur's pigeons the previous year.

'I'm worried, Tig. Remember what happened to Fevvers.'

Tig continued to stride onwards, her fingers coiled around his hand. 'Herc, the Festival did not kill Fevvers – that's stupid. Birds don't live very long. It was his time. If you're going to die of old age you do it in your nest, while you're asleep. You don't suddenly drop out of the sky and into the tombola.' Tig's jaw clenched. 'Look. I don't care what Arfur told you, Fevvers did not die of boredom.'

Their con-man friend may have helped save their lives a few months earlier and was still loyally keeping the secret that they were living all alone up at St Halibut's, but he was also in the habit of winding them up.

'Arfur says a lot of things. If you believe half of them you're even less brainy than his pigeons. Now stop moaning and try to have fun.'

As they walked on to Sad Sack High Street, it quickly became clear that fun was going to be in short supply. Bickley Brimstone, owner of the pharmacy and President of the Sad Sack Business Association, organized the Festival every year, though it wasn't clear exactly what there was to celebrate about the town's miserable existence. Mainly, the event seemed to be about forcing everyone to spend more money in his shop.

Bickley got very offended if the townsfolk didn't attend the Festival. If you stayed away he would give you the wrong change, accidentally shut doors in your face, and drop heavy things on your foot for the other 364 days of the year.

It was for this reason that Tig had insisted all the orphans at St Halibut's should attend. The last thing they wanted was Bickley taking a hostile interest in them. The people in Sad Sack hadn't noticed – or if they had, they didn't care – that the matron, Miss Happyday, had not been seen for months; she'd never exactly been popular. But that didn't mean the orphans could be careless. They'd already had a narrow escape. DEATH – the Department for Education, Assimilation, Training and Health – might look the other way if they heard rumours about St Halibut's, but if someone like Bickley Brimstone discovered the truth and shoved it in their faces, DEATH would probably feel obliged to do something about it.

'This is the worst festival in the whole world.' Herc kicked a stone at the *Welcome to Sad Sack* sign propped up against a bin, and it fell face-down in the dirt.

Tig didn't disagree. It was one of those events that looked a lot better on the flyer than it did in reality. The promised 'Fun Pool' was one of the bigger potholes on the high street, filled with dirty water; the 'Helter Skelter' was run by a sullen teenager who took a penny off you and then gave you a shove down the spiral iron staircase outside the Mending House.

Herc had no right to moan, really. True, the first weeks after the matron's death had been tricky: Tig, Herc and their friend Stef had come close to losing St Halibut's and spending the rest of their lives in the Mending House. Its Guvnor, Ainderby Myers, had threatened their very lives. But Herc had accidentally blown a huge hole in the side of the Mending House and they'd escaped. Bizarrely, this had resulted in Tig banning him from playing with any more substances from the pharmacy, rather than recognizing his clearly exceptional chemistry skills.

Still, all the poor Mended children had been rescued and Myers would never be seen again. At first, for a few weeks they had all lived together at St Halibut's, a riotous crowd of around forty that could make the windows rattle with their noisy games. But Arfur had pointed out that, unlike the St Halibut's children, most of the Mended were not orphans, and he had insisted on tracing their families. One by one, he had returned them to their joyful and surprised parents in every corner of Garbashire, saying simply that they had completed their sentences at the Mending House. There was no mention of explosions, or rescues, and the Mended children themselves were sworn to silence.

It was the right thing to do, Herc supposed, resentfully. But all the same, he missed them – especially because now he was back to being the youngest. Just the six of them remained: him and Tig, of course, plus their friend Stef, then Nellie and Cuthbert, the two St Cod's orphans they had picked up along the way, and finally Ashna, the Mended burglar. They were only four or five years older than him, but the way they acted sometimes, they might as well be his grandparents.

The day dragged on and on. Each shop had a stall outside it, decorated with miserable-looking bunting, as well as their usual wares inside. Herc searched for Ma Yeasty's stall, which would be the only one with something entertaining going on, and a snack or two to eat. He found her bakery stand being manned by Arty Chokes, the greengrocer, instead. Arty was busy removing sweet treats from the display and replacing them with what from a distance looked excitingly like severed heads, but on closer inspection were rows of wilted, sad-looking cauliflowers covered with mould spots.

'Where's Ma Yeasty?' Herc asked, unable to hide his disappointment.

Arty frowned at him. 'Gone for a lie down. Just as well if you ask me. Look at this – donuts! Disgusting. You can even *see* the sugar on them – she tried to tell me they were just dusty. She must think I was born yesterday. That woman has a blatant disregard for the health of our fine citizens.'

Herc gazed at the donut-filled bin behind the stall, his mouth watering. 'Oh.'

Ma Yeasty had told him of her plan for the stall: she had been going to run a 'Guess the weight of the cake' competition and hoopla, with donuts to throw instead of wooden rings. You could eat any that landed accurately on the pegs. And, knowing Ma Yeasty, any that didn't as well. It was the only thing about the Festival he'd been looking forward to.

He spent the next hour wandering sulkily through the streets as the summer sun dimmed gradually, every now and then checking his pulse in case he was, in fact, breathing his last and going the same way as Fevvers. He waved at Sue Perglue as she sat wretchedly at her hardware stall, half-heartedly advertising a contest to win a small packet of sandpaper. Unsurprisingly, few people had taken her up on the offer.

Maisie, the much kinder replacement Guvnor of the Mending House was proudly showing off all the knitted items made by the new young residents – scarves and gloves were festooned across her stall in a riot of bright colours.

DEATH still sent wayward children to the Mending House for punishment and re-education, but since Maisie had taken over from Ainderby Myers, life inside had changed somewhat. Whereas the previous Mended children had woven and spun cotton till their fingers bled, Maisie had her new recruits sitting around a cosy fire on beanbags, chatting, laughing, and knitting. She refused to call them Mended, except on the paperwork; to her, they were the Poppets. She sold whatever they produced and used the money to care for them as best she could, which was a *lot*: every night, she tucked each Poppet into bed and read a bedtime story while they sipped hot cocoa. It was all very nice, but the St Halibut's orphans preferred their freedom.

'How're you getting on with that hat, young man?' Maisie called to Herc as he passed.

'Oh, fine, thanks,' he called back, and walked a little faster. Since Pamela, their angry pet goat, had eaten most of their cash, the orphans had started to earn money by knitting for Maisie, after a few lessons. Some had taken to it more than others. Cuthbert had produced a number of chic cardigans using advanced stitches he'd looked up in the Crafts section of Arfur's mobile library; Ashna had managed a single, wonky scarf; Stef had accidentally stabbed himself in the stomach with a knitting needle while making a blanket that consisted mainly of a large hole; and Herc's bobble hat had never made it past the bobble stage.

Bickley Brimstone's pharmacy had a queue of people around it and Herc spotted Nellie watching from a short distance.

'He's still doing that swindle with the tea,' she told him, sounding both disgusted and admiring at the same time. Bickley Brimstone had been trying to sell a load of some mysterious herbal tea for weeks now, but no one had bought it. He had begun claiming not only that the tea would cure any sickness, but that he could tell people's fortunes from the tea-leaves, all for a pound a time. This seemed to be working much better as a sales tactic. Nellie shook her head at the queuers. 'I'll tell yer fortunes, ya wallies! You're gonna get a lot poorer. There ya go, that'll be a quid, mate.' She held out her palm to the nearest man, who obligingly rummaged in his pocket for a coin.

Before he could hand it to her, she was bundled away swiftly by a very tall boy with a scar that puckered the skin from his nose to his neck.

'Hey! Whatchya do that for, Stef?' objected Nellie. 'There's a great big bunch of stupid right there, easy pickings. They'd probably even buy that knitted hole you made.'

Stef gritted his teeth at her jibe about his knitting, but let it pass. 'The whole reason we're here is to keep Bickley happy, Tig said. You can't steal from his customers.'

Nellie snorted. 'He won't know. He ain't even been here most of the day. And now he's in his back room, making 'em drink that stuff and waving his hands over the dregs.' She wiggled her fingers as though performing magic.

Cuthbert and Ashna sauntered up to join them. 'Nellie dear,' Cuthbert reproved her. 'I've told you before – you really can't just go up to people and con them out of their money.' Stef nodded vigorously in agreement; Cuthbert was well-versed in legal matters. 'You need to get them to sign a piece of paper first, saying whatever happens next is all their fault. *Then* you can con them.'

Ashna shook her head ruefully. 'Honestly, you two. You're two sides of the same coin.'

Cuthbert shrugged. 'I'm the shiny side, at least.'

'Let's find the others and go home,' Herc whined.

'I'm tired and there aren't any donuts. Besides, my marshmallows will be set by now.'

'I suppose we done our duty. And it *is* getting late,' Nellie agreed, glancing at the sky, which had indeed turned a dingy grey. 'The sun's setting.'

'Don't be daft,' Stef told her. 'It just *feels* like we've been here all day. It can't be much past midday, yet.'

'Well what's that then?' said Herc, pointing triumphantly at the orange tinge on the horizon.

Stef's face was suddenly bloodless, as though his heart had fallen into his boots.

'That's no sunset,' Ashna said, her voice strangled.

The others turned as one towards their home.

A red-orange glow spread across the sky, a large plume of smoke forming boiling dark clouds above, blotting out the sun.

St Halibut's was on fire.

Chapter Two

'I looks a bit burnt,' Herc observed, as they stood at the very edge of the driveway of St Halibut's the following morning.

Burnt, thought Stef, *was an understatement.*

Their home was little more than a pile of ashes, broken bricks and stones still smouldering here and there. He could see familiar shapes – the iron bath, blackened and warped; an empty picture frame that had once housed the holy cheeks of St Halibut herself. There was no sign of the huge wooden dining table, or any of their beds. They must be among the tiny embers and ash floating around them.

This morning it had been right here – solid and forbidding and . . . home. Stef shuddered – they were lucky that none of them had been inside at the time.

There was a cough beside him, and he turned, drawing Herc's scarf back up over the boy's nose and mouth, trying to think of something comforting to say. But Herc was peering curiously at a small object he was holding between finger and thumb, misshapen and blackened, crumbling at his touch. 'I *think* it's a bit of marshmallow,' he was saying, his voice muffled by the scarf. 'But I suppose it could be anything. What if it's a cupboard handle or something? I don't want to eat a cupboard handle.'

Stef sighed. Part of him wanted to shake Herc and ask him if he really didn't see the trouble they were in? They had nowhere to go and just when they thought everything was perfect, all was lost. There was only desolation and despair for them now. But desolation and despair never seemed to know quite what to do with Herc. He tended to ignore them until they went away again. Now he knew that Pamela was unharmed, he seemed quite content.

The goat's shed was destroyed – probably a flying spark from the main fire – but not before Pamela had broken out. She was still wearing a short splintered plank on her horns, bashing Stef in the ribs every time she turned her head, and was refusing to let anyone take it off, as though it were a favourite hat.

'I *reckon* it's a burnt marshmallow. Do you think I can still eat it?' Herc asked. 'Or might it be poisonous now?'

'Best not.' Stef watched Cuthbert and Nellie wandering aimlessly on the other side of the rubble like lost souls. They were picking amongst the ruins, trying to see if anything could be salvaged. Ashna had stayed below in Sad Sack, because smoke was bad for her damaged lungs, and Tig was keeping her company.

They needed to stick together now, more than ever.

But that was the problem.

They had taken shelter in the Mending House last night but it was obvious they couldn't stay longer. Despite Maisie's protestations that she'd look after all six of them, it was painfully clear that there was simply no room. The dormitories were packed full to bursting already, bunk beds stacked to the ceiling because Maisie couldn't say 'no' to a child sentenced for Mending; if she didn't take them, another Mending House would, and that was a fate no one deserved. Lately, however, saying 'yes' had become literally impossible. It turned out that when you tried to fit three to each bed, two of the occupants ended up falling out. And when they fell onto someone else, because there was no space on the floor either, things got a little heated. There had been fights.

Last night, Stef had wandered around trying to find a clear surface to sleep on, and had finally nodded off inside a broom cupboard, leaning against the doorframe along with a mop, which in the morning had turned out to be Cuthbert, who'd had the same idea.

He felt tears prick his eyes; a small, warm hand slipped

into his. He looked down into Herc's face.

'It'll be all right, you know,' Herc told him solemnly, with a certainty that nearly broke Stef's heart in two. 'We're going to—'

'Uh oh,' Nellie's voice broke into his thoughts. 'Here comes the Crooked Chemist.'

Stef looked where she nodded and his heart sank. Bickley Brimstone's pointy head popped up as he climbed the last few steps to where they stood.

'I heard that,' Brimstone puffed. He hadn't been up the hill for many months and clearly didn't have the stamina for it. 'I was about to commiserate with you, offer my sincere condolences for your loss; there's no need for rudeness. What has happened here is a real tragedy.'

Stef gave Nellie a warning look to quell the sarcastic remark he could see forming on her lips. 'Thanks. We appreciate it, don't we?'

Cuthbert stepped forward briskly and stuck out his hand. 'Ever so kind of you.' Bickley shook it reluctantly as though it were a wet fish, while Stef gazed at his friend admiringly. Cuthbert's wealthy parents had taught him things like table manners and talking posh – skills that Stef had never really been able to see the point of, but at times like this they really came in handy.

Bickley's gaze slid expectantly over to Nellie. After

a long, mutinous silence, she dredged up a tight smile and a nod so tiny it could only have been seen under a microscope.

'Arfur told me the news about Miss Happyday,' Bickley said.

Stef tensed. No doubt Arfur had spun Brimstone a story that hid the fact that the matron had been dead for months, but there was no way of knowing exactly what he'd said. Had he told the pharmacist that she had died in the fire?

'Yeah. It's so sad,' he said, sadly.

'Terribly, awfully sad,' agreed Cuthbert. 'That poor woman. Such a pity.'

Bickley frowned. 'A pity? Suddenly winning thousands of pounds in a beauty contest and abandoning you all for a stellar modelling career? And to do so on the morning of the fire, thereby escaping it! I'd call that an incredible stroke of luck, wouldn't you?'

Arfur had proved himself a true friend, covering for them endlessly. But sometimes he liked to test just how gullible people were. It seemed he hadn't yet reached Bickley's limits.

'Oh, that, yes,' agreed Stef. 'Well, best of luck to her.'

'Never thought she was much of a looker, myself,' said Bickley, who had never seen anything as gorgeous as the handsome devil that greeted him in the mirror every day. 'Anyway,' he glanced between the children. 'I came up to let you know that your ride is here. Better not leave them waiting.' He gestured down to the bottom of the hill. Where the steps levelled out to the path that led into Sad Sack, there was a large, black-covered carriage attached to a pair of glossy horses.

Stef's skin went cold. Nellie and Cuthbert moved to stand with them and looked down.

'That's a . . . DEATH carriage,' Cuthbert said, blankly.

'Yes. I took the liberty of informing them of your tragic situation. They have found places for you all to live.'

Stef felt Nellie's fingers clutch at his arm.

'Together?' she whispered.

'Don't be silly,' Bickley laughed. 'No, you will be scattered across the country.'

Stef was stunned into silence. Bickley must have put pen to paper to tell DEATH almost the moment the first flames appeared. He stared at the pharmacist and a horrible realization uncoiled in his gut.

It would have taken at least two days for any message to reach DEATH HQ from Sad Sack.

Bickley had not sent it as soon as the fire started.

He had sent it before.

About the Author and Illustrator

Sophie Wills grew up in Chelmsford, Essex. She failed the 11+, had a weekend job at a boarding kennels where she suffered workplace bullying from a goat and nurtured a dream to have a career she could do in her pyjamas.

She entered Mumsnet's first Bedtime Story competition in 2012 and Michael Rosen picked out as a winner her story about a pig-riding sheriff.

She lives on the edge of south-east London with her family.

David Tazzyman is an internationally acclaimed, award-winning and million-copy bestselling illustrator. He worked as a commercial illustrator before falling into children's publishing in 2006, illustrating Andy Stanton's Mr Gum series which went on to win numerous awards, including the first Roald Dahl Funny Prize in 2008. Now David mainly illustrates children's picture and fiction books and lives in Leicestershire with his partner and three children.